MIRACLE

AT

THE MISSION

ENDORSEMENTS

Looking for the perfect blend of relatable characters, fascinating history, intriguing mystery, and strong faith? Look no further than Miracle at the Mission. Author Joseph Lewis' vivid descriptions of the California coast will sweep you away on this epic adventure.
—**Leslea Wahl**, award-winning author of The Perfect Blindside and other successful faith-based novels for teens.

Joseph Lewis is a talented author who has succeeded hugely with Miracle at the Mission. Readers will quickly recognize the work as a combination of the Hardy Boys, current geopolitical events, and the reclamation of the saintly Spanish missionary, Junipero Serra. When you turn the final page you think: if this doesn't bring our youth back to the faith, what will?
—**Brian J. Gail**, best-selling author of the American Tragedy in Trilogy series (Fatherless, Motherless, and Childless).

Very Timely... Joe Lewis has a true knack for taking a timeless, traditional world and pulling forward into the present culture. This sequel is an easy, wonderful read for all. Truly a MUST read for anyone who attended an all-boy prep school. In the busyness of life today, it is nice to slow down with a book like this, let it resonate, and remember when ... Such a nice reminder, and I enjoyed the suspense!
—**Pete De Maio**, husband & father of seven, President of PA for Human Life, Speaker, and Business Owner

MIRACLE

AT

THE MISSION

JOSEPH LEWIS

ELK LAKE PUBLISHING INC
PUBLISHING THE POSITIVE
Plymouth, Massachusetts
A Christian Company

COPYRIGHT NOTICE

Miracle at the Mission

Cover and Interior Design: Derinda Babcock, Deb Haggerty
Editor(s): Steve Mathisen, Cristel Phelps, Deb Haggerty

PUBLISHED BY: Elk Lake Publishing, Inc., 35 Dogwood Drive, Plymouth, MA 02360, 2022

Library Cataloging Data

Names: Lewis, Joseph (Joseph Lewis)

Miracle at the Mission / Joseph Lewis

210 p. 23cm × 15cm (9in × 6 in.)

ISBN-13: 978-1-64949-566-2 (paperback) | 978-1-64949-567-9 (trade paperback) | 978-1-64949568-6 (e-book)

Key Words: Mystery; Junipero Serra; California Missions; Russians; Assassinations; Lost Gold; Inspirational

Library of Congress Control Number: 2022937808 Fiction

DEDICATION:

To my children, David, Julia, Audrey, Daniel, Stephen, and Evelyn. Thank you for your love, support, and patience. Your mom and I are truly blessed to have each one of you in our lives and are so very proud of you. We love you very much!

ACKNOWLEDGMENTS:

Many thanks to Leslea Wahl, Nikos Lambdin, Don Mulcare, Nancy Yates, Russell Huneke, and Susan Peek, all of whom have been so kind in offering their assistance in the reading and editing of all or parts of the book, or in providing their expert advice and suggestions. You are all wonderful people, and I am extremely grateful for your help in making the book the best it could be.

To the fine people at Elk Lake Publishing, especially Deb Haggerty, Cristel Phelps, Steve Mathisen, and Derinda Babcock. Thank you for your professionalism, consideration, and good cheer. You truly make the process of publishing a book a lot of fun. I hope we can do this again sometime soon.

A special thanks goes to my daughter, Julia Lewis Lennox, who has become a very talented editor in her own right. Your ideas and recommendations did much to improve the book and for that I am extremely grateful. Thank you for making an already proud father even prouder!

Above all, I want to thank Theresa Linden. Theresa is an award-winning author who asked me to send her the first chapter of my manuscript many months ago. From that point on, she freely offered her time and assistance in helping me not only grow as a writer but in refining what I thought was a good story into a novel. Theresa, your kindness and generosity in offering your guidance and expertise throughout the process is beyond measure. I cannot thank you enough for all you have done in helping make this book a reality. I am eternally grateful. God bless you.

PROLOGUE

Adrik Chernov took a sip from a cup of steaming hot tea. After many years of hard living, it had become his drink of choice, the strongest beverage to pass his lips in several months. He stood on the balcony of a villa overlooking the Black Sea in the resort town of Gelendzhik in Krasnodar Krai, Russia. An associate had invited him to stay there as long as he liked and enjoy all the amenities a place like this had to offer—walks on the beaches, the pleasant sea breezes, a swim in the pool.

He had looked forward to this time in his life, to be able to retire and finally live as he pleased. This would be the perfect place to do it. All the arrangements had been made. The house would be his, and he would be able to take on an assumed name and disappear forever as if his previous life had never existed. The money he needed to make it all possible stared him right in the face. If he accepted this one last assignment, the payout would far exceed any amount of money he had ever dreamed of.

His phone buzzed on the table next to the chaise lounge behind him like it had been doing for the last hour. He would only be able to ignore it for so long. The people calling him needed an answer.

As an expert marksman and one of the most highly-skilled, long-range snipers in the world, his skills had made him a highly valued commodity. He excelled at his craft and did it with precision and efficiency. He never thought much about the consequences of his work. The people who stood in the crosshairs of the scope of his rifle meant little to him. He merely followed orders, completed his assignment, and collected his pay. All in a day's work.

Call him a professional assassin, a hired gun, a hitman—it didn't matter what term you used. He had chosen the life, and he was good at it. But the job had also taken its toll on him, always on the run, lurking in the shadows, living under numerous aliases, never able to simply relax and do what he wanted to do. Instead, he longed for a life of leisure.

He stared at the phone from across the balcony. The offer these people made would allow him to do just that. But had he tempted fate for too long? Every assignment had its risks and dangers. He had often played with fire and had come close to getting burned. With every escape from near disaster, the odds increased against him. Had his time run out?

But he also had to face reality. With his money tight, he had to think about the future. An opportunity like this might never come along again. The thought of finishing his career a rich man and never having to look back finally urged him across the balcony. He picked up the phone and made the call.

After little more than an hour, a knock at the front door revealed a package left on the outside welcome mat. He had been told in advance of its delivery. Inside he found a falsified passport, cash for expenses, and information about where the job would take place—California. Though it had been many years since his last visit, he knew that getting in and out of there would not be overly complicated, given how open the southern border of the US had become in recent years. He also had contacts there he could count on.

Following standard protocol, further instructions and information about his target would not be revealed until later. The kind of money these people agreed to pay him, however, suggested it had to be someone of considerable value.

He returned to the balcony with another cup of hot tea. By now, the sun had begun to set. A glowing sphere of fire slowly dipped beneath the horizon of a deep gray sea—low-lying clouds reflected colors of red, blue, purple, and orange. It was a scene he hoped to return to and experience again, many times over. But first, he had one more job to do.

CHAPTER 1

Pete Figueroa stepped into the Westthorpe Academy auditorium. Getting there late, he worried he had missed the big announcement. Cheerful voices filled the air, most just above a whisper but some louder. He glimpsed a few of his classmates, their parents, and siblings sitting with them. He noticed only a couple of seats remained empty. He'd better find one soon. Where was—

"Hey, Pete, over here."

Pete looked toward the voice.

His best friend, Joe Pryce, waved him over. He was sitting with a couple of their sophomore classmates. "Where ya been? I thought maybe you weren't comin'?"

Pete took a seat next to Joe. "Did I miss anything?"

"Well, as a matter of fact, you did." Joe glanced toward the stage. "Clayton Starks just won the Perfect Attendance Award in our class for the second straight year. Can you believe it?" A grin slowly came to Joe's face.

Pete frowned, not the least bit amused. "Come on, you know what I mean."

"Oh—you must mean the big announcement!" Joe put an arm around Pete's shoulder. "Not to worry, pal, it looks like you got here just in time."

As if on cue, voices suddenly quieted as Father Al Sarjinski stepped to the podium. Father Al (short for Alfons) doubled as chaplain and theology teacher at the all-boys Catholic high school. Not to mention he was an all-around good guy. He'd become somewhat of an institution at Westthorpe, having been there many years, even as a student.

"I want to thank you all, again, for coming to our end-of-the-year closing ceremony." Father paused, looking out toward the crowd. "And now, the moment we've all been waiting for! I would like to announce the winner of a very special award."

Pete fidgeted in his seat, struck by a sudden sense of anxiety. He took in a breath, his heart pounding faster in his chest.

"As many of you know, several of our students this year participated in the Serra International Essay Contest, where students from around the country were invited to submit an essay on why the life of Saint Junipero Serra was important to them." Father Al had helped encourage students to get involved in the contest. Serra International was a lay organization named after Saint Junipero Serra that helped promote and support vocations to the priesthood and religious life.

"I wish he'd just get on with it," Pete mused.

"I also want to take this occasion to thank Mr. McAuliffe, chairman of the history department, for his assistance in helping encourage and guide the students in writing their essays."

Several students had responded to Father's challenge, including Pete and Joe. They both became interested in Saint Junipero Serra's life after following the events of his canonization a couple of years previously. Pope Francis came to the United States and oversaw the official canonization ceremony at the Basilica Shrine of the Immaculate Conception in Washington, DC. It marked the only time in history when a saint had been canonized in the United States.

"And a special thanks to our Headmaster, Dr. Nichols, for allowing us to participate in the contest and for his leadership and moral support." Polite applause followed from the crowd as Dr. Nichols waved and smiled from his chair next to the lectern.

Pete could hardly stand the suspense any longer. The anticipation had all started last week when Father Al shared the news that a Westthorpe Academy student won second place in the essay contest and that he would reveal the name during the closing ceremony. Pete had always enjoyed doing research and crafting a good paper or putting together an impressive PowerPoint presentation. But, as much as he liked the thought of winning the contest, he wasn't sure if he really had a chance, especially with all the other guys in school who also submitted essays.

"I still think you're the man to beat," Joe whispered reassuringly. Joe was the one who had encouraged Pete to participate in the contest. He was the kind of friend you could always count on for moral support and a boost of confidence. He had reminded Pete of how well he did on term papers and thought he had as good a chance as anyone. "I didn't want to tell you this," Joe said, leaning toward Pete, "but I made a bet with Tim Doolittle that you would win."

"Doolittle bet against *me*? How could he? I thought we were friends!"

"I wouldn't make anything of it. I gave him odds he couldn't refuse."

"And that's supposed to make me *feel better*?!"

"Shh ... Father's about to tell us who the winner is."

"Of the many essays Serra International received from all over the country, it is my pleasure to announce that the second-place winner is ... our very own ... Pete Figueroa!"

Pete's jaw dropped, and his eyes almost jumped out of his head.

Thunderous applause erupted throughout the auditorium. Students immediately surrounded Pete, slapping him on the back.

"Didn't I tell you?" Joe shouted as he gave Pete an enthusiastic high five.

After recovering from the initial shock, Pete bounded his way up to the stage and shook hands with Father Al and Dr. Nichols. He could hardly believe it. He looked at the certificate and the check he received. Yeah, it must be real—they both had his name on them. Still, it was going to take a while before it all sank in.

Pete returned to his seat to more applause. "Way to go, dude! Let me take a look at that." Joe snatched the check from Pete's hand. "Wow, seven hundred and fifty bucks! Looks like both of us won some money today!" He paused, then looked out across the auditorium. "Hey, it looks like Doolittle is trying to leave without paying what he owes me." Joe jumped up from his seat.

"You can tell him for me he bet against the wrong guy," Pete said.

"With pleasure—after I collect my money. Then we can celebrate with ice cream at Handel's. I'm buying." Joe spun and headed toward the exit doors of the auditorium. "I'll be right back."

The next day, Joe and Pete headed back to school to meet with Father Al. He had invited them to lunch and said he had something he needed to tell them.

Pete gripped the steering wheel of his father's Ford Taurus. He had just recently gotten his license and was more than happy to drive them over.

After arriving around noon, they made their way through the empty school halls, past the cafeteria, and into Moreau Hall, the oldest building on campus. The faculty dining room was normally reserved for faculty and staff, so Pete felt especially privileged to be there.

"Hi, Pete! Congratulations on your award. We were so happy for you!" Mrs. Kostopoulos, officially known as the Food Services Director of the school but more like another mom to all the students, carried a tray into the dining room.

"Thanks, Mrs. K., I appreciate it."

Mrs. Kostopoulos was a woman of strong faith who repeatedly told the boys how she always prayed for them, especially after the extraordinary events that occurred at the school just a year ago.

"Well, there they are!" Father Al stepped into the dining room wearing his black clerics with a short-sleeved shirt but without the white priestly collar. Father was heavyset and wore glasses. He always seemed a bit disheveled, with his shirttail always sticking out a little, his thinning grayish-brown hair not quite combed right. But it was all part of his charm. As a priest, he possessed a gentle demeanor while always remaining solidly committed to the truths of the faith. He was a friend to everyone who knew him.

"Hello, Father. We've got a nice lunch for you today," Mrs. Kostopoulos announced.

"It sure looks good, Mrs. Kostopoulos. Is that your famous macaroni salad?"

"I made it especially for you, Father—and the boys, of course. I'll leave you three to your lunch. Let me know if you need anything else. God bless you."

Both Joe and Pete thanked Mrs. Kostopoulos as she left the room.

"I appreciate you fellas coming by today, especially after such an exciting evening last night." Father directed the boys to the silverware and drinks at the end of the counter. "I've got to tell you, Pete, keeping your award a secret sure wasn't easy. Needless to say, I wanted to share the news with you long before the announcement."

"I don't know how you did it, Father," Joe said. "Did anyone else know about it?

"Well, to tell you the truth, that's part of why I invited you both to stop by."

Never one to hesitate in matters of food, Pete stepped up to a tray resting on top of a buffet table and helped himself to an Italian hoagie and a generous portion of the macaroni salad. After they all sat down at the table, Father Al led them in grace.

"To be honest, Father," Pete said as he finished blessing himself, "after this week, I don't know how many more secrets I can handle." He picked up his hoagie. "But don't get me wrong. A nice lunch like this can only help."

"I hear you, Pete. And don't worry. What I've got to share with you is all good news." Father took a swig from his Snapple lemon iced tea. "I have a proposition for the two of you." He wiped his mouth with a napkin. "As a result of your exceptional achievement, Pete, you've been invited to attend this year's national convention of the United States Council of Serra International in California. You will be honored along with the other essay winners from around the country.

"Wow—are you kidding?" Pete's eyes widened, stunned by yet another surprise. "California? My brother Luke is out there!"

"The trip will also include a special event at the nearby Mission San Carlos Borromeo of Carmel, one of the original missions founded by St. Junipero Serra." Father eased back in his seat, noticeably enjoying the excitement he had generated. "And rumor has it the president of the United States has been invited to attend the same event as part of the celebration honoring the two hundred and fiftieth anniversary of the founding of the mission there—delayed these last couple of years due to COVID restrictions."

Father pushed his chair out and sauntered across the room toward the dessert table where Mrs. Kostopoulos had put out an assortment of cookies. "Serra International will cover the flight and hotel stay for you." He stopped and glanced at Joe. "And, after consulting with the leadership of my order, they have also agreed to invite Joe to go along with you—all-expenses paid."

"*Really*?" Joe coughed, almost choking on his food.

"Consider it part of a gesture of appreciation for what both of you have meant to the school."

Pete hardly knew what to say. For some time now, Father Al had been telling them how the school wanted to show its appreciation for their heroic efforts of last year. Not only did the boys find a considerable amount of money that had been buried on the school property for many years, but they also helped nab a couple of fortune-hunting thieves who had tried stealing the money. The school had faced financial difficulties, and the money helped save it from being forced to close.

Joe slurped down some of his drink, then cleared his throat. "Hey, Father, does this mean I might have to sit next to this guy on a long flight like I had to do when we flew down to Orlando last summer? Always getting up to go to the bathroom, moving around, never keeping still."

"Yeah, listen to you!" Pete could hardly believe what he heard. "As *I* remember, you were an *invited guest* of the family at the time. Plus, you couldn't stop talking about how much of a good time you had."

Father shook his head. "People would never know you two were best friends."

"We are, Father." Joe grinned. "We're just busting on each other."

"Well, I'm glad to hear that." Father sat back down in his chair. "Because there's even *more* to tell." He finished swallowing a bite of his cookie. "It just so happens that I've been planning a trip of my own to visit a priest friend of mine who lives in Oregon. He and I plan to fly down to California to meet up with you guys."

"Cool! That sounds even better, Father." As soon as Pete had said this, he suddenly remembered his family and what they might think of all this. Would it disrupt their plans for the summer?

"And not to worry," Father added as if reading Pete's mind. "We've already contacted both your families several days ago, and they have given an enthusiastic thumbs up to the idea."

"Several days ago?" Joe echoed. "Then they must've known about Pete's award all this time."

"And so has his brother Luke." Father smiled. "In fact, he's already made arrangements to take leave during the time you guys are there. He happens to be stationed in Monterey, which is right where you'll be."

"Are you kidding, Father?" Pete clasped his hands in back of his head as he leaned back in his chair, still trying to process it all. "I can hardly believe all this."

"It sounds like the perfect trip, Father." Joe glanced at Pete. "You'll have to thank the superiors of your order for us."

"The trip is scheduled for the last week in June, so you still have a couple of weeks to get ready."

Pete reached over and gave Joe a fist pump. "California, here we come!"

CHAPTER 2

The president removed his reading glasses and placed them on his desk in the Oval Office. "Is there anything else, Ned?"

Edward "Ned" Marin, special adviser and strategist to the president, glanced down at the notepad resting on his lap. "Sir, there is one last thing I'd like to bring up." He paused to clear his throat. "Aside from the many important matters related to the upcoming G7 Summit in San Francisco, I wonder if I might ask if it is not too late for you to reconsider your options concerning the mission event afterward in Carmel?"

Marin had waited to near the end of the meeting before broaching the subject. Well aware of the president's reputation for an unwavering determination once he had committed to something, a trait Marin often admired, he knew this would not be an easy task. However, recent events had convinced him that circumstances had changed enough where he needed to express his concerns to the president in the strongest possible terms.

The president pushed himself away from the desk and eased back in his chair. "Go ahead, Ned. I'm listening."

"I'm sure I needn't remind you, Mr. President, of the important political implications surrounding this issue." Marin leaned slightly forward in his chair. "Your presence at the Carmel Mission is bound to be viewed by many as controversial, not to mention the protests it is sure to encourage. We are already facing an international situation with Russia that still remains uncertain. Since replacing Vladimir Putin, President Tarasovich of Russia has given some indications of wanting to restore their membership in the G7, and possibly attending this year's summit, despite the economic sanctions still imposed upon his country."

"I'm sure that's part of his motivation," the president said, rather tersely. "But as long as a single Russian tank remains in Ukraine—regardless of their ongoing military withdrawal from the region and promise to pay war reparations—I don't see how any of the member nations could agree to it, including ourselves." He pointed to a newspaper on top of his desk. "As much as the world welcomes regime change in Russia, their continued testing of hypersonic nuclear missiles, and the threat to use them, is still a major concern. Not to mention their ongoing denial of cyberattacks we know originate from within their own country." He paused. "I'm afraid the Russians leave us no other choice but to keep the sanctions in place. We must continue to demonstrate a posture of strength and unity, both among our allies and at home."

"That is precisely why I think your attendance at the mission event may not be the best idea," Marin replied. "The whole world is watching. Any sign of a perceived weakness, such as a possible protest against you at the mission, especially with the G7 Summit as a backdrop, will surely be used as propaganda. China, North Korea, Iran—as well as Russia—would like nothing more than to project an unfavorable impression of you and your policies, both here and abroad—not to mention the heightened security risk this will no doubt cause, including that of your own safety."

There, he had said his piece. He had laid out the facts to the president as best he could articulate them. Whether it resonated or not, he would have to see.

The president remained silent for a moment before gazing up at Marin. “I certainly understand your concerns, Ned. I’ve been thinking about this ever since we received the invitation from the California Missions Foundation and the good Franciscan friars there, as well as the bishop of Monterey.”

The president stood and turned toward the large windows behind his desk. The late afternoon sun brought soft rays of light through the open curtains and into the Oval Office. “How I do wish our country could come together on matters that should unite us rather than divide.”

Returning to his desk, he slouched back in his chair, the weight of his responsibilities palpable. “Goodwill among peoples, as well as among nations, is a cherished thing, but rarely ever easy.”

“True indeed, Mr. President.” Marin paused, hoping a breakthrough had occurred, and that the president might be coming around to his point of view. “Perhaps, then, we can agree that going to the Carmel Mission may not be in the best interest of furthering that same goodwill we all desire.”

The president began tapping his fingers lightly on top of his desk, studying it closely. “I’m sure you must know something about the history of this desk, Ned?”

Marin nodded his head, rather surprised, though, by the president’s question. “Of course.” He gazed at the desk, examining it from end to end. “It’s the famous Resolute desk, given to the United States as a gift from Great Britain, as I remember.”

“That’s right.” The president placed both his hands on the top of the desk. “But what most people don’t know is how this desk helped prevent a war.”

“Hm. I must admit to being one of those people,” Marin confessed.

The president smiled. “The *Resolute* was a British ship that became trapped in the ice filled waters of the

Canadian Artic in the mid-1800s, its crew lost. The ship was later recovered by a group of American fishermen and, after a complete overhaul, sailed back to England with an American crew where it was presented to Queen Victoria herself. Recognized as a gesture of goodwill and a desire for peace, both the Americans and the British softened their demands over a Canadian border dispute, averting an almost certain war.

"Many years later, they greatly honored the *Resolute*." The president sighed. "Honored her for her service to exploration and as a symbol of peace and goodwill among nations. When she was eventually retired, the Brits decided to salvage part of her valuable timber for the making of at least three desks." The president patted his hand on top of the desk. "One of those was given to the president of the United States at that time, Rutherford B. Hayes, as a special thanks for the rescue and return of the *Resolute*. This revered desk has been used by practically every president since then and has become a fixture in the Oval Office."

The phone on the famous desk buzzed, and the president reached across to answer it. "Yes ... I haven't forgotten ... thanks for letting me know. Please tell everyone I'll be there shortly."

The president put the phone down. "We promised our grandchildren and various nieces and nephews we would take them to see the musical *Aladdin* this evening at the Kennedy Center. That's a constituency I dare not disappoint," he said with a broad smile.

"For me, Ned, going to the mission is also an opportunity to honor an important national symbol that has much to do with the formation of our country." He glanced again at the desk. "Not unlike the *Resolute* was for Great Britain, the story of the California missions belongs to our heritage and holds a significant place in our history as a nation. And, perhaps more importantly, the missions are places of religious worship and spirituality for the thousands of people who visit them every year."

Marin could detect the momentum he thought he had gained earlier suddenly reversing course. He knew he would have to scramble to retrieve it. "I certainly don't dispute any of those things, Mr. President, and I greatly respect the religious conviction of those who value the missions even beyond their historical importance, including those of your own Catholic faith. However, my concern is for those who don't view the missions as you have described. As you know, some see the missions as symbols of colonialism and oppression."

"I understand that, Ned, and I am sensitive to those convictions and respect those who hold them. But I also see this as an opportunity to provide a forum for dialog. And isn't that what our country is supposed to be about? Might this be an opportunity to discover the true legacy of the missions and of their founder, Saint Junipero Serra?"

"I would agree with that, Mr. President, but wouldn't another occasion at a different time and place be a more appropriate opportunity for such a discussion?"

The president glanced at his watch.

"I don't mean to hold you up any more than I already have, Mr. President."

"Don't be silly, Ned. I'm the one holding *you* up." He grabbed the phone again. "Hello, Dianne, I'm about to wrap things up here. Unless the chief-of-staff has anything further he needs to discuss with me today, please tell him I'll see him first thing in the morning. Very good, thank you."

The president hung up the phone. He stood up, angled around his desk, and sat in one of the front chairs adjacent to Marin.

"Ned, I'm sure we can talk further about this in the days leading up to the trip." The president looked directly at Marin. "But for now, let me leave you with this. As you know, they found one of the original mission bells that had been lost for many years. They've invited me to be there for the unveiling and ringing of the bell. Throughout their history, the bells have been of prime importance to the missions." The president paused. His eyes narrowed as he stared intently at Marin. It was an expression those around the president knew all too well—that what he was saying, he meant with the utmost conviction. "This is truly a momentous and solemn occasion that means much to our country's history and religious heritage. And I am honored to be invited to be a part of it.

"And, of course, who can't help but appreciate the irony of it all." The president eased back in his seat as a wry smile came to his face. "The bell they found had originally been a gift to the mission from the Russians who also established a settlement in Northern California during the same period. As you know, the original plan for this event called for a celebration of goodwill and cooperation at the mission, with both the president of Russia and me in attendance. Unfortunately, with the development of recent events, all that has changed. Nevertheless, I do believe my presence there can help bring attention to the effort of preserving the missions and honoring an important legacy of the history of our country."

Marin nodded his head approvingly. "Mr. President, there is no doubt of your sincerity in wanting to support such a worthy cause. However, I'm sure I needn't remind you of the recent events that have occurred involving the defacing of statues, and particularly those of Saint Junipero Serra himself, as well as acts of vandalism at several of the missions he founded throughout California. I'm sure you must have heard about the burning of the church at Mission San Gabriel in Los Angeles." He paused. "Perhaps waiting until things settle down might be the more prudent thing to do."

The president sat quietly, staring across the room as if allowing himself to take in everything they had talked about. "I appreciate your concerns, Ned—I really do." He turned in his chair. "But I prefer to think that regardless of whether any progress can be made in furthering a more enlightened discussion of this issue, at the very least, this can be an opportunity to demonstrate clearly that the tearing down of statues and the damage to private property, particularly in our places of worship, is simply unacceptable."

"On that, Mr. President, we can agree. But part of my job is to offer my advice on how things are perceived through a political lens. With that in mind, I would hope you would at least consider letting others in the administration be out front on certain issues—this being one of them—while you continue offering your leadership and support."

The president stood up and started moving toward the door of the Oval Office that led to the main corridor of the West Wing. Seeing it as a signal for the conclusion of the meeting, Marin followed the president to the door.

The president stopped and turned toward Marin. "Ned, I don't see how a single visit to the Carmel Mission to celebrate Mass and to honor the work of the Franciscan friars can be much cause for concern. Besides, since when have you ever known me to back down from a challenge?" The president opened the door. "At the same time, you do know how much I value your good opinion." As Marin passed through the doorway and into the corridor, the president placed a hand on his shoulder. "And I promise you, I will give this further consideration. Let's be sure to talk again before I leave." The two shook hands. "You know, Ned, perhaps the one thing I'm looking forward to the most about the trip is playing some golf at Pebble Beach. Please don't tell me you object to that."

"I suppose not, sir." Marin turned back toward the president and smiled. "The only advice I could offer you there would be to hit 'em straight."

The president laughed. "I'm actually feeling pretty good about my game of late. I'm going to try and play at a course up near Camp David this weekend—get a little practice in."

"Sounds good, Mr. President. Do enjoy your evening with your family."

"Thank you, Ned, and my best to yours. God bless."

The meeting had ended on a warm note which eased Marin's mind a bit. But as he headed down the corridor from the Oval Office, he couldn't help but worry that as much as the president appeared to have made some concessions, he still seemed determined as ever to go through with his plans.

CHAPTER 3

"Fantastic. A window seat!" Pete lifted his carry-on into the overhead compartment.

"Not so fast. That's my seat." Joe put his ticket right up to Pete's face. Suddenly, though, Joe thought about it. "But you know what?" He extended his hand out in the direction of the seat. "I'm gonna let you have it, knowing how you are on flights."

"You're not starting that up again, are you?"

"I'm being perfectly serious. But it's only a one-time offer."

"You're sure you don't mind me taking it?" Pete moved over a bit in the aisle as someone squeezed by him. "I'm happy to take the middle one."

"No, you're not. Nobody's *happy* to get the middle seat, especially on a five-hour flight." Joe scooted over to let Pete get by. "Besides, if you don't sit there, you'll be constantly leaning over me, looking out the window."

"You're probably right. Nothin' like watching the world from 30,000 feet." Pete slid across and settled into his seat. "Thanks, pal."

Joe threw his bag into the compartment above their seats then glanced over at Pete. "Are you sure you have everything you need from your bag before I sit down?"

Pete had already opened one of his books and yanked a pair of earbuds from a pocket of his backpack. "Oh, yeah, would you mind grabbing my water bottle on the side of my bag? Thanks for the reminder."

"Not a problem. Just promise me you won't drink too much of it, knowing how you like to get up and go all the time."

"I'm glad you brought that up." He stuffed a bookmark between pages. "I'd better take care of that now before we take off." Pete scooted back across the seats.

"I thought you went in the airport?"

"I did, but that was a while ago." Pete turned and headed to the rear of the plane toward the restroom.

Never a big fan of flying, Joe had been a little nervous on takeoff. But once they had leveled off above the clouds, he was fine. Pete seemed to enjoy every part of it. When not reading one of his books, he stared out the window, commenting on everything he saw. Joe smiled. He and Pete had been friends all the way back to elementary school at St. Philomena's. They had done practically everything together since. As much as Pete had his little quirks, Joe couldn't ask for a better friend.

Joe was happy to know Pete would see his older brother Luke, a lance corporal in the Marines. Currently stationed at the Presidio in Monterey, California, a US military installation—home to the Defense Language Institute, Luke studied Russian in an intense full-immersion program that prepared him for work in linguistic intelligence.

"Hey, Joe, did you hear? They're saying the president is gonna be at the Carmel Mission for the event we're going to!"

"No kidding! That's great!" Joe stuffed a magazine back in the pocket of the seat in front of him.

"Yeah, I saw it on the news." Pete scrolled down on his phone. "Here it is. He'll be in San Francisco for the G7 Summit but plans to visit the mission afterward."

Joe thought back to the dramatic events at their school that occurred just over a year ago when they found the money. The story gained national attention, even drawing notice from the president of the United States. The president sent his own children to Catholic schools and became particularly interested in the events at Westthorpe Academy. After seeing it on the news, the president invited Joe, Pete, and their families to Camp David, the presidential retreat outside Washington.

But there was more to the story than the extraordinary recovery of a lost fortune. Both Joe and the president, a convert to the Catholic faith, discovered they shared similar interests and devotions in the practice of their faith. Joe had given some hints that divine assistance had played a part in the mysterious circumstances leading up to finding the money. But there were only a few select people he felt comfortable enough discussing it with. Among them were Father Al and, ultimately a person Joe would have least expected, the president.

Since then, both he and the president had downplayed the matter and had chosen not to talk about it publicly. What they had revealed was their shared devotion to the Blessed Virgin Mary, especially under the title of Our Lady of Lourdes. Both visited Our Lady of Lourdes Shrine in Emmitsburg, Maryland, where the president liked to go during trips to nearby Camp David. Joe went to the shrine during a school trip with Pete and their classmates in the spring of their freshman year. While at Camp David, Joe and the president visited the shrine together.

After being in the air for a while, Joe finally dozed off. Suddenly, something shoved his elbow off the armrest, pulling him from his sleep. His head tipped forward, then jerked back, eyes snapping open.

"Sorry about that." Pete patted Joe's arm. "I was just shifting a little, trying to get comfortable. You weren't asleep, were you?"

"Of course not," Joe mumbled. He stretched his arms and yawned. "Just resting my eyes. Couldn't you tell?"

Pete was one of the few people on the flight who had the reading light on above his seat. A couple of books lay open on his lap as he leafed through one of them. Joe picked up one of the books and read the cover out loud. "*A Guide to Treasure in California.*" He looked up, his eyes squinting, his brows drawn down over them. "Exactly what are you planning on doing on this trip?" He set the book down and grabbed another. "*The Padre's Gold: The Search for a Hidden Fortune in the California Missions.*" Joe frowned. "Please tell me you aren't serious about this stuff?"

Pete grabbed the books back. "Hey, I'm entitled to do a little innocent reading. Besides, some of this is really cool. Did you know that geologists say there's still more gold to be found in California? Some say the real Mother Lode hasn't even been discovered yet!"

"And I suppose you're the guy who's going to find it."

"I'm just sayin' what the experts are telling us. Here, you've got to read some of this." Pete turned to a page in one of the books. "Did you know that the padres of Mission San Antonio de Padua are said to have helped run a silver mine many years ago? It was known to the locals as the *Priest Mine*. The silver ore was carried from the mine to the mission and stored there until it could be put somewhere else. They say not all of the silver was moved and might still be somewhere on the mission property."

"Uh-huh." Joe tried not to take too seriously another one of Pete's wild notions.

Pete leafed to another section in the book. "Here's one I really like. There's an area called Point Lobos near the Carmel Mission. They say the Indians of the mission used to sift through the black sand in the crevices of a cave near the sea there and guess what they found?"

Joe shrugged. "More silver?"

"No—gold! Some of it in large chunks. Wouldn't it be cool to explore a place like that?"

"Did I hear you say *Point Lobos*?" Joe asked, suddenly interested. "That's a place I also did some reading about before the trip. It's supposed to be one of the best parks in all of California. They say it's got some great trails and rock formations that jut out into the ocean with all sorts of wildlife like otters, seals, even whales."

"Then it's agreed." Pete gave a nod. "Point Lobos is definitely on the list. By the way, I'll bet you can't tell me when gold was first discovered in California."

"Of course, I can." Joe sat up straight. He prided himself on possessing a sound knowledge of history. "1848, John Sutter's Mill, discovered by a man by the name of James Marshall. When word got out, it started the California Gold Rush of 1849. That's where we get the term *49ers* from."

"That's what *most* people think, but they'd be wrong." Pete opened another book. "Listen to this. In 1842, a man named Francisco Lopez, a *majordomo* of one of the ranches of Mission San Gabriel—that's like a chief foreman or steward—discovered particles of gold clinging to the roots of some wild onions growing near an oak tree. Today you can still see the oak tree and a historical marker where the gold was found."

"Maybe we can go see it," Joe said, trying to humor his friend.

Pete looked down at his book again. "Within only a couple of years, miners had taken most of the gold from the hills there. Word spread that some of the gold had been given to the padres in the nearby Mission San Fernando Rey, and they hid some of it on the property. With no more gold left, some people decided to search through the mission for the *Padre's gold*, which, they say, was never found."

Joe grimaced. "Please don't tell me you brought your metal detector with you."

"I'm not saying I'm going to use it, but yeah, I've got it in my bag." Pete pointed to the luggage rack above them. "I called the airline, and they told me that, depending on the size, I could carry it on. It's a small model, and I was able to disassemble it with no problem."

Joe sighed. "You don't think we've already had our fair share of discovering hidden treasure?"

"Come on." Pete pushed his head back on his seat. "You've got to admit, what happened last year was pretty exciting. Besides, look at the good that came from it. It helped save our school, didn't it?"

"Yeah." Joe nodded his head. "But that was completely unexpected and kind of fell into our laps. And don't forget the danger we found ourselves in having to deal with a couple of criminals along the way."

"But I'm not comparing this to that. Who knows, maybe I'll just find an old coin, or someone's lost watch on the beach. Pretty innocent stuff. It's kind of a hobby of mine. Very laid back."

Joe could hardly argue with that.

"To me, it's just as much fun just searching for things, learning the history of where you are, even if I don't find anything." Pete took out his phone and started scrolling through it. "Last summer, I visited my uncle John down in Virginia, who really got me interested in metal detecting. He searches mostly for Civil War relics. He's got a really neat collection of stuff like bullets, medals, ID tags, swords, bayonets, belt plates, you name it. Here, let me show you some of them." He handed the phone to Joe.

As someone who liked history, Joe actually enjoyed looking at Pete's pictures. He couldn't blame him for pursuing something he really liked doing. Joe eased back in his seat. "Just promise me you won't go poking that thing around where it might get somebody in trouble."

But Pete had already put his earbuds in and opened another book.

MIRACLE AT THE MISSION

Joe and Pete moved briskly along the narrow corridor of the arrival gate in the San Francisco airport. A woman in high heels and a yellow dress suddenly squeezed between them, talking on her phone and pulling her luggage behind her. "Excuse me, excuse me." She rushed through to the next group of people in front of her.

A tall figure in uniform stood just ahead of them. He wore desert camouflage surplus and a matching flattop cap. He had a lean frame, and the sleeves of his shirt were folded neatly above the elbows of his arms. Words above the chest pockets became more visible, US MARINES on one side and FIGUEROA on the other.

Pete ran ahead. "Hey, Luke!"

Luke Figueroa walked up and greeted Pete with a wide grin and a big hug. "How are ya, little brother? Let me look at you." He backed out of the hug and gave Pete the once-over. "I think you've grown a couple of inches since I saw you last."

Joe came up behind them. "I'd say it won't be long before he overtakes you."

"Yeah, we'll see about that," Luke smirked. "Good to see you, Joe."

"You too, Luke." They shook hands. "How are the Marines treating you?"

"Well, you know. It's a tough job keeping the country safe, but somebody's got to do it."

"Hey, what's that under your sleeve?"

Luke pulled up his left sleeve even higher to near his shoulder, revealing a tattoo. It covered most of his upper arm and featured a winged figure with a halo surrounding its head. The figure wore medieval armor and held a large sword pointing straight down with the handle covering most of its face. "It's St. Michael the Archangel."

Joe studied it with fascination. "It's pretty cool."

"A couple of us decided to get one. With a middle name like Michael, it seemed like the right choice. The guy showed me one I liked."

Pete stepped back, his eyes widened. "Wow, have you told Mom and Dad yet?"

"Yeah, I sent them a picture." Luke lowered his sleeve. "Dad liked it. He reminded me his dad was a chief petty officer in the navy and had both his arms covered with tattoos." He paused. "Not sure what *Mom* thought about it."

They started walking.

Pete put an arm around his brother. "Well, ya know everybody at home says hello and sends their love."

"I sure miss seeing them. It's been too long since I've been home. But I'm sure glad you guys were able to come."

"We really appreciate you picking us up, Luke." Joe checked his phone. "Saved us an Uber fare."

"Not a problem. I've been looking forward to seeing you guys ever since my leave started right after PT this morning."

"PT? What's that?" Joe asked.

"PT stands for 'Physical Training,' right Luke?" Pete glanced toward his brother.

"You got it. Bright and early, 0500. After we finished, I had just enough time to jump in the car and drive here. What normally takes less than two hours from Monterey to San Francisco took almost three with rush hour traffic. Everybody drives in California."

"Yeah, but you've got to love the weather." Joe looked out through the large windows of the airport. A clear day with bright blue skies.

"You guys are here during a good time of the year. The winter and spring months can be pretty dreary with lots of fog. After I finish my training, I'm hoping to land my duty station at Camp Pendleton, near San Diego. That's the kind of California weather I like—sun and more sun."

Joe nodded his head. “Sounds nice.”

“Hey, let me treat you guys to a little place I know not far from here, where we can get a late breakfast—what do you say?” Luke glimpsed over at Pete. “I know Pete’s always hungry.”

“I’m starving,” Pete put his hand to his stomach. “All we got on the plane was some water and those crummy, thin cookies that taste like cardboard. Let’s go!”

After breakfast and driving from San Francisco, they finally reached Monterey, where Luke pulled up to a small park. Joe jumped out of the back seat and peered out toward the ocean. Boats filled a small harbor just below them. “Wow, what a view.” He imagined what it would be like to own his own sailboat and be able to take it out on the water anytime he wanted.

“That’s the Monterey Harbor and Marina, all part of Monterey Bay. We’ll have a chance to visit there later.” Luke turned and led them a few steps toward a statue with a black iron fence surrounding it. “This is where Saint Junipero Serra first landed in 1770 and celebrated Mass on this very spot.”

Pete looked at Joe. “How cool is that?”

“A famous oak tree used to be here, marking the site where the Mass took place.” Luke pointed to where the tree had been. “Part of it is now located at the Carmel Mission, not far from here.” He peered up at the statue. “Unfortunately, this was vandalized around the time of his canonization, but it’s been restored.”

Joe carefully studied the simple white statue. The figure of Saint Junipero Serra looked out over Monterey Bay. Priestly vestments rested over his habit, his right hand was raised in benediction, and a peaceful expression graced his face. Why would anyone want to destroy this statue of a humble and holy man who wanted nothing more than to bring the message of God's love to the people he served? Joe read part of the inscription on a plaque just beneath the statue.

> IN MEMORY OF FATHER JUNIPERO SERRA, A PHILANTHROPIST SEEKING THE WELFARE OF THE HUMBLEST, A HERO DARING AND READY TO SACRIFICE HIMSELF FOR THE GOOD OF HIS FELLOW BEINGS.

"This is all part of what is called Lower Presidio Park." Luke pointed toward the other side of the statue. "Behind us and up the hill is the Presidio of Monterey, what I currently call home."

"This is such a neat place." Pete raised his head in the direction of the Presidio. "Dad always said the Marines could have sent you somewhere a whole lot worse."

"I won't argue with that." Luke took a glance at his watch. "Hey, we probably oughta get going. I'll show you guys around Monterey a little bit, and then we'll head up to post. I need to stop by my barracks and change my clothes." They started walking back to the car. "After that, I'll take you guys to the best deli sandwich place around—Campagno's. It's not far from here. You need to check out their desserts. Best cannolis in town!"

They made the short drive to the downtown district.

"That looks like one of the missions right there." Pete pointed to a church on the other side of the street they had turned onto.

"You're right, Pete." Luke pulled over and stopped the car along the curb, just in front of the church. It was a beautiful building with large archways and portals carved into its sandstone walls. A large bell tower stood to the left of the entrance. The façade featured a small alcove at the top that held a statue of Our Lady of Guadalupe underneath a large simple cross.

"This is the San Carlos Cathedral, also known as the Royal Presidio Chapel of Monterey," Luke explained. "It was the very first mission in the Monterey area—built by Father Serra not long after he arrived. Later, he relocated the mission further away from the Presidio and moved it to Carmel—Mission San Carlos Borromeo of Carmel. It's not far from here. It became the headquarters of all the missions in California that Serra started. That's where we'll be for the dedication in a couple of days."

From there, they drove further into town, where they visited the famous Monterey Aquarium and Cannery Row, and then down to the waterfront along Old Fishermen's Wharf. After a while, they hopped back in the car and headed toward the Presidio.

Luke pulled up to the gate entrance. A soldier, wearing camouflage surplus with US ARMY on his front pocket and a black beret cap, stepped toward the car. Luke showed him his identification. "Have a nice day, gentlemen." He signaled for them to proceed through the gate.

"This is actually an Army facility." Luke turned the wheel into a parking lot. "All the military branches send their personnel here for foreign language training, but only a few Marines are in any of the programs."

Luke parked the car in front of a set of buildings that Joe guessed were barracks. "Home, sweet home," Luke announced. Joe and Pete followed Luke inside. Although it had beige-colored cinderblocks for walls, Luke's room seemed comfortable enough. It had everything in its proper place, a pair of black spit-shined shoes set squarely on the floor, bed covers meticulously folded and tucked under the mattress. But aside from that, it did surprise Joe to find Luke's living quarters looking more like a college dorm suite than the austere and Spartan-like military barracks he had envisioned.

After changing his clothes, Luke walked them over to some other buildings where most of his classes were. "Yeah, it's an exciting life here, let me tell you. I go to class, study, get something to eat, study some more, sleep a little, go to class ... I'm living the dream." He flashed a smile.

"What do you do when you're not going to class or studying?" Joe asked.

"What little downtime I have, I like to get over to the fitness center here on post. Maybe we can go over there later. This afternoon, though, we'll head down to Mission San Antonio, and hopefully, get checked in.

"Mission San Antonio?" This was news to Joe.

"Not to worry, fellas." Luke put an arm around Pete. "We registered a little late for the convention and weren't able to get a room at the hotel there. The best they could do was put us on a waiting list. That's when I thought about Mission San Antonio de Padua, which is a little further down the El Camino Real, the road that connects all the missions of California. It's one of the few missions that has overnight stays with cloistered rooms just like those Junipero Serra and his Franciscan friars experienced when they lived there."

"*Cool!*" Pete's face lit up. "It sounds like the perfect place! I did some reading about Mission San Antonio, and the book talked about how there might still be a hidden deposit of silver there."

"Oh, no." Joe shook his head at Luke. "You've got him going now. That's all he talked about on the flight. Stories about more gold and silver to be found in California."

"I'm familiar with some of those stories," Luke said. "Though you can't believe everything you hear—or read about." Joe was grateful to hear at least that part. "A few years ago, a couple, not far from here, found one of the greatest buried treasures ever discovered in the US. They were out walking their dog and saw something sticking out of the ground. They went back and got their metal detector and found some rusty cans filled with gold coins worth ten million dollars!" Luke tapped his phone and scrolled down. "Here it is. It was called the Saddle Ridge Hoard."

"Wow!" Pete grabbed Luke's phone and stared at the screen.

"Nobody knows for sure how it got there, but it wasn't unusual for people to hide treasure like that to keep it from being stolen." Luke smiled. "Of course, you guys know something about that with what you found at your school last year."

They had walked back to the barracks and turned toward the parking lot. "Back when California was still a wild frontier, there weren't too many places to keep things like that, so people buried them instead." Luke touched the button on his key fob and unlocked the car. "Problem was sometimes the people died, or they forgot exactly where they buried their stash."

"Exactly." Pete looked up for a moment from Luke's phone. "I'll bet there's a lot more like that to be found,"

"Be careful what you read, though," Luke warned. "There can be a fine line between fact and fiction. A lot of legends have sprung up over the years about the Old West that makes for great entertainment."

"Did you hear that?" Joe glanced over at Pete. But Pete remained focused on Luke's phone and either didn't hear him or simply chose to ignore the question. "For me, I'd love to go to the mission just to have the experience of seeing what life was like for the original friars and Saint Junipero Serra himself." Joe was hoping to move the conversation in a different direction. But he was also genuinely interested in finding out about the monastic life at a mission. He visualized himself in a Franciscan habit, working and praying with the friars. "Wasn't Mission San Antonio one of the earlier missions Serra founded?"

"Yeah, and he spent a lot of time there," Pete said as he handed the phone back to Luke. "Like I said, it's the perfect place for us to stay."

“Well, I’m glad to know you’re paying attention after all,” Joe said with a wry smile.

Luke jammed his phone back in his pocket. “I tried calling them a couple of times but never spoke to a live person. It’s located in probably the most remote area of any of the missions.” He opened the driver’s side door. “They don’t seem to have a booking service online either, so I left a message on their answering service about reserving a room and when we were coming.” All three jumped back in the car. “I figured we’ll just drive down there and check it out.”

Pete’s stomach gave a conspicuous growl. “Sorry about that, but I’m starving. What about lunch?”

“Don’t worry, I haven’t forgotten.” Luke started the car. “First stop—Campagno’s—and then we’re off to Mission San Antonio.”

Joe had to admit he liked how the trip had suddenly taken on an element of mystery and adventure. Going to one of Saint Junipero Serra’s missions and not quite knowing what to expect actually sounded like fun. Maybe Pete was right. A little excitement and intrigue on a trip like this couldn’t hurt anyone. Besides, after what they experienced last year, what could possibly top that.

CHAPTER 4

Lunch at Campagno's turned out to be everything Luke had promised. To Joe's surprise, Pete struggled to finish the exceptionally large Italian sub he had ordered. But that didn't stop him from grabbing a cannoli for the road before they jumped back in the car and headed for Mission San Antonio.

After almost an hour, they pulled off the highway onto a dusty secondary road. Having passed a few neighborhoods and shopping strips earlier, they had reached a much more rural area with rolling hills and purple mountains in the distance.

"This region is called the Valley of the Oaks—mostly farms and vineyards out here." Luke started working the brakes more as the road became winding and narrower. "This mission is more inland than most of the others. And being in an isolated location, it doesn't get as many visitors ... which is probably a good thing for us." Luke turned slightly to avoid a large ditch in the mostly unpaved road. "There are some cool places to see down here besides the mission. You've got the Big Sur, which isn't far—"

Pete interrupted. "Yeah, I was hoping we'd get a chance to go there. It's supposed to be one of the coolest places to see in California."

"We're also not far from the famous Hearst Castle," Luke said, "built back in the 1920s by publishing tycoon William

Randolph Hearst. In its heyday, it was the place to go if you were among the rich and famous. Today, it's owned by the state of California and open to the public."

Suddenly, a large truck pulling a military tank on a trailer swept by, very close to the car, going in the opposite direction.

"What was that?" Joe twisted in his seat to look behind them.

"That's another thing I meant to say." Luke glanced in the rearview mirror. "There's an army reserve installation down here called Fort Hunter Liggett, used mostly for tactical field training and joint military exercises. It's a surprise for most people who visit this place. When the Army first came here many years ago, it actually did a lot in helping restore the mission. It's pretty much the same way it's looked since the eighteenth century. As long as Uncle Sam is here, hopefully, it'll stay that way."

Luke slowed as the road turned and led to a wide opening. Just ahead, Joe could see the white adobe-brick structure of a Spanish mission rising from the road ahead. As the car moved closer, the distinctive Spanish-tiled red roof came more into focus, resting atop a long series of lower archways extending far to the left. A larger building stood off to the right—probably the mission church or chapel. A large bell hung in a center alcove at the very top, with more of a grayish light-brown façade and three archways below.

"Welcome to Mission San Antonio de Padua," Luke announced as he brought the car to a stop in a mostly-gravel and empty parking lot. "Although it's been a while since I've been here, it's the kind of place that never seems to change. It's probably closer to the way it looked at its founding than any of the other missions."

"I can't wait to look around." Pete flung his door open and jumped out of the car.

"Not so fast." Luke climbed out, turning toward Pete. "Let's make sure we can get checked in first."

An older woman with tanned skin and long dark hair strode toward them, coming from the mission buildings—almost as if she had been expecting them. She wore deer hide moccasins, a long skirt, and a shell necklace. After greeting them with a smile, she motioned for them to follow her. She was extremely pleasant but spoke very few words, using what sounded like a mix of Spanish and another language Joe did not recognize. She communicated with them using mostly gestures.

She led them down a long outdoor corridor. The woman stopped, swung open a door, and motioned to Luke that this was his room. Luke smiled and peeked his head inside. "Yeah, it's perfect. Thank you for being able to accommodate us."

The woman then glanced from Joe to Pete, motioning for them to follow. She cracked open the next door over.

"Thanks." Joe stepped inside first. Light streamed in under a half-drawn blind, falling on one of the two twin-size beds. A fresh linen scent filled the air.

Pete followed. He walked over to a small table that had an old-fashioned basin with a large pitcher sitting inside. A towel was laid next to it. "Do you think they have running water?"

"If they don't, I guess we'll get a feel for what life was like for the friars and the native people who once lived here."

"I just hope they have modern bathrooms."

Joe glanced back outside to thank the woman, but she was no longer there. "Hey, look." He picked up a piece of paper on the end table between the two beds and read aloud the handwritten note. "*You are invited to 5:00 p.m. Vespers (evening prayer) in the mission chapel. Dinner is at 6:00 p.m. in the refectory*."

Pete stared wide-eyed at Joe. "Did you say *dinner*?"

"Yep—but only after prayers."

After settling into their rooms, the boys ventured outside. Joe enjoyed looking at the many artifacts found all around the grounds, each telling something of the history of the place. The original well, grist mill, and a fascinating aqueduct system all dated back to when the mission was founded, according to markers placed near each of them. A large old oak tree drew Joe's attention. He imagined it must have been very young when Saint Junipero Serra first came here.

He ventured to the rear of the property and found the mission cemetery. A marker described the site as the final resting place for many of the people of the Salinan Indian tribe who helped build the mission. The marker further explained that at its peak, the mission numbered well over a thousand Indians who lived there.

Luke came up behind Joe. "The last time I visited here was for what they call 'Mission Days,' an annual fundraiser and celebration of the mission." He looked out over the low adobe wall that surrounded the cemetery. "Descendants of the Salinan people come here to honor their ancestors and proudly recall their history and heritage with the mission."

They walked back toward the main buildings of the mission. As Joe turned a corner, a group of Franciscan friars, maybe six or seven of them, in long gray habits and sandals, strolled through the courtyard. He didn't think anyone else was there. The friars kept their distance, each in what appeared to be their own private reflection and meditation, like a silent retreat.

After the boys returned to their rooms for a little relaxation and a short nap, they headed over to the mission chapel. Joe stepped inside, touched the holy water in the font near the door, and made the sign of the cross. The fragrance of incense and the sweet aroma of lighted candles filled the air.

They proceeded down the center aisle toward the sanctuary, wooden pews on either side of the long nave of the chapel. Beautifully colored trim adorned the white adobe walls. Carefully laid oakwood planks ran the length of the high-angled ceiling. Just in front of the sanctuary, a wide archway touched the ceiling and curved down along both sides of the walls. Painted blue with gold trim and dozens of stars, it reminded Joe of the mantle worn by Our Lady of Guadalupe.

The same Franciscans they had seen earlier knelt on both sides of the center aisle near the front, now about fifteen of them, with one standing and signaling for the boys to join them there.

As they walked up, Joe could see more closely the simple but beautiful altar and sanctuary, which featured several statues, including St. Francis of Assisi, St. Michael the Archangel, and, of course, St. Anthony of Padua. Statues of the Blessed Virgin Mary and St. Joseph stood on either side, with a painting of Our Lady of Guadalupe on the left wall. The chapel also featured decorative paintings Joe discovered were done by the Indians who had once lived there long ago.

The boys settled into a pew just behind the friars and pulled down the kneeler to pray. The monks wore their hoods pulled over their heads, all looking alike as they knelt quietly before the altar.

Suddenly, everyone began to stand, marking the beginning of the liturgy with the sign of the cross, followed by the reciting of a prayer.

> "O Lord, in union with that divine intention with which you rendered your praises to God while on earth, I desire to offer this my prayer to you. Amen."
>
> A prayer of thanksgiving followed.
>
> "How shall I be able to thank you, O Lord, for all your favors? You have thought of me from all eternity; you have brought me forth from nothing; you have given your life to redeem me, and you continue still, daily to

pour your grace and blessing into my life. I praise you. I bless you. With all the Saints, I praise you.

"Almighty God, have mercy on us, forgive us all our sins through Our Lord Jesus Christ, strengthen us in all goodness, and by the power of the Holy Spirit keep us in eternal life. Amen.

"Pour down your blessing, O Lord, on your whole church, on the Franciscan Order and all the Brothers, Sisters, and Companions of the Order. Help the poor, the sick, and the dying; comfort the lonely and the abandoned.

"Have mercy on this community and grant that humility, peace, and charity may rule therein. Grant that we may love and serve thee faithfully all our days. Through Our Lord and Savior Jesus Christ. Amen."

A time for quiet meditation and private prayer made up the last part of the service. Joe found himself greatly moved by the whole experience. He had listened intently to each of the words of the prayers. They seemed to speak to him. But as much as they brought him a genuine serenity and inner peace, there was also a sudden awareness of something else—a strange mix of apprehension and urgency he couldn't quite understand. He quickly dismissed it as something that had somehow found its way into his consciousness. He turned his thoughts, rather, to an appreciation for the place they were in—where Saint Junipero Serra once lived and prayed with his small group of Franciscan brothers and the many indigenous people of the area. He made a special point to give thanks for his many blessings and to pray for the intentions of his family and friends.

The sound of a bell ringing from atop the chapel snapped Joe from his quiet reflection. He glanced at his phone—six o'clock sharp!

"That's got to be the dinner bell," Pete said in a low voice.

"Just relax," Luke whispered. "We'll go when the friars go."

Almost on cue, the Franciscans removed themselves from their pews. Each one genuflected before the tabernacle and strolled to the back of the chapel.

"No faithful monk can resist the call of a resounding mission bell," Luke whispered, "especially when it summons them to mealtime." After waiting their turn, the boys also genuflected and proceeded out the door of the church to the dining facility.

They arrived just in time, as one of the friars led everyone in a blessing of the meal. Immediately obvious was that the friars' observance of silence extended to their meals as well. Out of respect, the boys found a table far enough away where they would not disturb them.

The meal was served by the same woman who had greeted them when they first arrived. She was assisted by a couple of the friars who mainly served their fellow brothers. Though Joe assumed there must have been other staff members on the premises, he had not seen anyone else.

As they were staying in a place more inclined toward spirituality, austerity, and simplicity, which Joe appreciated as part of the experience, a delicious dinner with all the fixings came as a complete surprise. There was chicken, fish, rice and potato casserole, freshly baked bread, and salad, followed by lemon cake for dessert. After dinner, they were given what the woman referred to as *Champurrado*, a traditional chocolate drink, served hot and right out of a copper pot at their table. She used what she called a *molinillo*, a handcrafted wooden whisk-type utensil, to stir the rich, creamy drink to a froth at the top.

"So *that's* what those are used for," Luke said. "I've seen those sold in shops out here but never knew what they were."

Pete took a sip from his cup. "I read about this in some of my research for my paper. It was a favorite drink of Saint Junipero Serra." He licked his lips. "It was one of the few luxuries he allowed himself to have ... and you can see why."

Joe also took a sip. "Did you know chocolate originated in Mexico many centuries ago?" He looked at Pete, not wanting to be outdone with the history lesson. "It was served mostly as a drink and wasn't even made into a solid form until much later." He took another taste. "When the Spaniards brought chocolate to Europe from the Americas, it wasn't popular until the Spanish friars introduced it to the king of Spain."

When the woman walked by again, Pete asked if they could have more of the chocolate. She indicated to him that after having served the friars, none of it was left.

Luke sighed. "Oh well. We can hardly fault them for that. I'm sure had Saint Junipero Serra been here, he would have approved of his brother friars liking something he couldn't resist himself." Luke stood up from the table and stretched. "Not that I had room for more chocolate anyway—that was some dinner." He patted himself on the stomach.

The woman pointed to a nearby cart where the boys put their dishes and silverware.

"Thank you very much—everything was delicious," Joe said. The woman nodded and smiled.

"You know, Pete," Luke said, "with all your reading about finding lost gold and silver, I've got something to show you I think you'd be very interested in seeing." He moved toward the door. "Come on, you two —let's go for a walk."

Luke led Joe and Pete along a path not too far from the mission. Joe watched his steps carefully as they reached the edge of a ravine and stopped at a spot overlooking a relatively shallow river and the small valley it flowed through.

"When I visited here before, I remember this being a great place to see the sunset." Luke pointed toward the horizon. "The taller mountain there is Junipero Serra Peak, the highest elevation along the Santa Lucia Mountain Range."

As the sun dipped behind the mountain tops, a beautiful array of red, orange, and pink hues painted the western sky before them. Joe took in the view. "Ahh, God's majestic handiwork. You can sure see why Saint Junipero Serra chose a spot like this for the mission."

Luke pointed across to the opposite side of the river. "And over there is an old, abandoned silver mine."

"Really?" Pete turned and gazed out in that direction. "Where?"

"If you look really closely, you can just make out a cut in the rock where the entrance was."

Joe strained his eyes and spotted a small, dark opening along a crevice, mostly covered by brush, weeds, and other ground cover.

"Nobody knows for sure when it was first used, but it was probably abandoned long after the missionaries were here," Luke explained. "They say there's a couple of these scattered around the area."

"That's really cool!" Pete began scanning the terrain below. "Is there any way we can get down there and take a closer look?"

"Please tell me you aren't serious," Joe implored.

Luke shook his head. "Not something I would advise doing. There's always the danger of cave-ins—not to mention rattlesnakes and other things in some of those old mines that don't like being disturbed."

Pete continued staring out at the old mine. Joe remembered him talking about the possibility of a hidden deposit of silver still being found on the San Antonio Mission property. He figured seeing the old mine must have triggered Pete's imagination.

"Hey, Pete, let's go," Joe called out to him. "We're heading back."

"What? Oh, yeah, I'm coming."

After returning to the mission, Joe and Pete followed Luke into his room. "We've got a long drive ahead of us tomorrow," Luke said as he sat down on a chair. "Father Al is flying down from Oregon early tomorrow and plans on meeting us at Fort Ross, not far from San Francisco."

"What's at Fort Ross?" Joe asked.

"It was a Russian settlement up until about the mid-nineteenth century." Luke put his feet up on the bed. "It's now a historical landmark and state park. We're going to the Fort Ross Festival, which is held there every year." He moved his head from side to side, glancing at both Joe and Pete. "Knowing how you two like history, I think you'll enjoy it. And, Petey, they serve great food there too."

"*That's* what I was waiting to hear." Pete stretched out on Luke's bed, with his hands behind his head.

"The festival is really unique." Luke stood up and emptied the contents of his pockets onto the desk next to the bed. "It celebrates the Native American and Russian history and culture that existed side by side there two hundred years ago. Father Al's friend is a priest of his order and teaches history at the University of Portland. His expertise is in Native American studies, and he invited Father Al to attend this year's festival with him. It seemed like the perfect place to meet up."

"It sounds pretty cool," Joe said.

"And, on top of that, I get to work on my Russian with people that speak it fluently. Our instructors are always encouraging us to look for opportunities like this."

"You know," Pete said, "it's almost like this whole trip was meant to be—the way everything seems to be falling into place—as if it were more than just coincidence that we're here."

"It *is* kind of strange." Joe sat on the edge of the window and looked at Pete. "Think about it. Father Al had already planned on being out here. Then you win the contest that brings us here at the exact same time. Not to mention how your brother Luke was already here—and then we hear the president himself is going to be at the mission ceremony we're going to."

"What are you two driving at?" Luke stared at them with one eyebrow raised, his forehead scrunched. "You sound like a couple of conspiracy theorists."

"I'm just saying, it seems like more than a coincidence these things have come together the way they have, almost like there's some purpose behind them," Pete said. "But don't get me wrong— I like to think it's all for the good."

"Amen to that." Joe looked at the crucifix on the wall above the bed. "The Lord is always looking out for us."

"On that, we can all agree." Luke glanced at his watch. "Hey, it's time to get some sleep. We've got a big day tomorrow. I'll see you two in the morning—bright and early."

Joe and Pete went next door to their room and settled in for the night. After a while, Pete still had the light on next to his bed, reading one of his books. "Hey, Joe, you still awake?"

Joe had just started falling asleep. "Barely," he murmured. He gave out a long yawn. "What's up?"

"I've been thinkin' about that old silver mine Luke showed us."

Joe struggled to stay awake. "Yeah?"

"What if the mission sat on a whole stockpile of hidden silver—or maybe even gold? The place doesn't seem to attract much attention. Maybe nobody's ever bothered to really look the place over. What would it hurt to do a little poking around?"

"Hm." Joe turned in his bed and fell sound asleep.

Joe opened his eyes. He felt for his phone on the nightstand next to his bed. It read 12:48 a.m. Though it was dark, enough dim light from the window fell onto Pete's bed. He wasn't there. Maybe he had gone to the bathroom. Feeling the need to go himself, Joe slipped into his beach sandals, opened the door, and started down the corridor.

Not finding him in the bathroom or back in the room, Joe decided to look around outside. Their room was one of several along a traditional Spanish-style portico that opened onto a large, quadrangle-shaped central patio and courtyard. Stars filled the night sky in a way Joe had never seen before. It provided the only light as he looked around and began calling out Pete's name in a hushed voice. No one responded.

He walked across the patio, passing a large fountain and some fruit trees, and headed toward the front of the mission, hoping to find Pete there. After walking around for several minutes, he turned back and proceeded toward the chapel. He slowly opened the door and peeked inside. The only light within came from the red sanctuary candle next to the tabernacle on the altar and a couple of votive candles underneath the statue of Saint Joseph to the right.

Joe genuflected and began walking down the center aisle. After taking a few steps, he stopped short—his breath suddenly caught in his throat. Just ahead and to his left, a figure sat on the far end of a pew directly beneath the portrait of Our Lady of Guadalupe. Regaining his composure, Joe stepped quietly, not wanting to disturb whomever it was. He drew closer and looked again. The person's clothing became more visible—a gray Franciscan habit. *It must be one of the monks from the retreat.*

The figure turned toward Joe. The hood of his habit covered most of his face as he bowed his head. "Good evening, my son, and may God be blessed." He spoke with a Spanish accent, his deep voice making him seem older. His manner gave Joe the impression that he was a priest.

"Good evening, Father," Joe said, "I didn't mean to disturb you."

"You haven't, my son. I am pleased to have your company. *Por favor*, I invite you to join me."

"Thank you, Father, but I'm afraid I can't. I'm looking for my friend Pete. You may have seen him with me and another guy earlier. The three of us are together. Luke is the taller one. He's Pete's older brother. Pete's got dark hair. Anyway, he and I are sharing a room, and he got up sometime during the night, and I can't seem to find him." Joe glanced around the dim chapel. "You don't recall seeing him anytime this evening, do you, Father?"

"Your friend is blessed to have such a faithful companion as yourself." The old padre spoke in a gentle but serious tone. "A good friend is something that should always be cherished in one's life."

"He's a good friend, all right, but sometimes he gets some crazy ideas in his head." Joe paused. "Now that I think about it, that's probably what he's doing right now." Joe pictured Pete stumbling around in the dark, searching for a hidden stash of gold or silver he'd convinced himself was somewhere on the mission property.

"*Sí te entiendo*," the padre said, "I understand."

"Thank you, Father, but I think I know now what my friend might be up to. I very much appreciate your kind words. I'll go see if I can find him. Thank you again for your help."

"Before you go, my son, I should tell you that just before I came to the chapel, not long before you arrived, I did see what appeared to be a young man walking toward the guest quarters. He wore a hood over his head, so I could not determine his features. However, he did seem to be carrying something like a staff that was rounded at the end. I don't know if that is of any help to you."

Joe remembered that Pete had been wearing his hoodie earlier that evening, and Father had just described what sounded like Pete's metal detector. "I think that might be him, Father. I can't thank you enough."

The padre turned and looked at Joe. The hood of his habit had opened wider, revealing more of his face. In the dim light, his eyes looked dark and his complexion a somewhat lighter olive brown. His thinning gray hair was cut in the traditional *tonsure* style, something more common among religious orders in the past but not as much today. He wore a large crucifix that hung underneath his hood and rested over the top front of his habit.

As Joe prepared to leave, he suddenly stopped, though he wasn't sure why. Something of what he had experienced earlier that day in the chapel seemed to compel him to want to listen to what the old padre had to say. Joe slid closer across the pew, sitting just a few feet from him in the pew.

"I am confident you will find your friend safe," the priest said in a reassuring voice. "From what I gather, the three of you are here for an extraordinary week. So much of what is going on in the world today has found its way near to this very place. Important leaders will be meeting, and the eyes of the world will be watching. It is no coincidence that, at this time in history, they have come here, where so many peoples and cultures met not very long ago and welcomed the missionaries who brought the message of the Gospel. It was, and continues to be, a message of the love of neighbor, of joy and forgiveness, of thanksgiving for one another, and peace among all nations."

Joe sat mesmerized. Though the padre referred to present-day events, his eloquent words and profound meaning made him seem like someone from another time, another world.

"But there are forces in the world that oppose these cherished things. Principalities who are enemies of God and of mankind, who choose the darkness; some who are visible and made of flesh and blood, others who are spirit and lurk in the shadows." He paused as he looped the rosary beads he had been holding in his hand through the cincture around the waste of his habit. "My son, the world's current dangers are real and require the courage and effort of a select few whose work can make the difference between conflict and resolution, division and harmony, hostility and goodwill for all peoples. The events of this week are crucial in determining the direction the world may be inclined to go. We must pray for God's Divine Providence, that those who lead us may choose the path of peace. Look for the signs of God's guiding hand in answer to those prayers. I also want to implore you and your friends to be vigilant this week, as you will be close to many of these things. The world can be a dangerous place, and sometimes people find themselves in circumstances they could hardly have anticipated."

"I very much appreciate your concern, Father." Joe politely accepted the padre's advice, although he didn't quite understand why he felt the need to offer it. But this wasn't what Joe had come here searching for. He still didn't know for certain if Pete was all right. Joe stood up. "I better get back and make sure my friend is okay."

"*Sí te entiendo.*" The padre grabbed hold of the back of the pew and pulled himself up. As he did, he shifted as if to favor one leg. He had a thin frame and couldn't have been more than an inch or two over five feet. His worn sandals looked as though they had traveled many miles.

"Please don't get up on my account," Joe said.

"I wish to extend to you my priestly blessing, my son." With some effort, he shifted his legs again and moved a little closer to Joe. "I am extremely glad you and your friends can spend some time with us in this beautiful place. You know, the mission is in great need of support to help maintain it, not only to preserve the legacy of the missions but for the work they continue to do. This mission is an active parish and serves many people and families, some of whom are descendants of the native people who first lived here many years ago. Please keep the missions, and the people they serve, always in your prayers, won't you?"

"I will, Father." Joe turned to leave but turned back again. "I sure hope we have a chance to talk again. I've really enjoyed our conversation."

"So have I, my friend, so have I. God willing, we will have a chance to meet again. In the meantime, go in peace."

The padre raised his right hand and extended it toward Joe, who bowed his head. "*Heavenly Father, I ask you to bless this fine young man and his companions in all their endeavors. May their work bear much fruit in the service of your kingdom. I ask that you protect them and keep them safe from harm in the name of Christ, Our Lord and Savior, Amen. May the blessing of Almighty God, Father, Son, and Holy Ghost descend upon you and remain with you forever. Amen. Amar a Dios, mi hijo*. Love God, my son ... and may He make a saint of you!"

"Thank you, Father." Joe slid back across the pew, then genuflected before the tabernacle. He pivoted and glanced back at the old padre, but he wasn't there!

Joe looked around the church. "Father?" There was no sign of him. Where could he have gone—and so quickly?

Joe headed back to his room, hoping the padre had been right about seeing Pete. He reached the door, opened it, and walked in. The room was dark, so he turned on the flashlight on his phone. Pete lay stretched out on his bed, sound asleep.

Joe climbed into his bed, thinking of the old padre and what he had said and how he seemed to mysteriously vanish into thin air. Suddenly feeling very tired, he closed his eyes and went to sleep.

CHAPTER 5

A pounding at the door pulled Joe from a deep slumber.

Knock, knock, knock! "Hey, guys," said a muffled voice from outside the door. "It's time to get up!"

He pulled a blanket over his head, trying to shield himself from the loud intrusion.

Knock, knock, knock! "You guys need to get up now so we can hit the road." The locked doorknob rattled.

"I'm coming," Pete groaned as he staggered from his bed and opened the door.

"Let's go, gentlemen," Luke boomed like a drill sergeant as he walked into the room. "We're driving to San Francisco, so we need to be on our way."

Joe was awake, but barely. He forced his eyes open, sat up, and took a deep breath, though sleep continued to beckon him. As much as he fought the urge, his body leaned, and he fell back on the bed again.

"*Somebody* I know was up searching for lost treasure," Joe said as he slowly sat up again and grabbed a shirt from his bag.

Luke turned a sharp glare at Pete. "Don't tell me you were out poking around with the metal detector."

"It wasn't for *that* long," Pete mumbled. "I couldn't sleep, so I went out for a stroll—no big deal. Don't worry. I didn't find anything anyway."

"I wouldn't advise using that unless you get permission from somebody here." Luke started rummaging through Pete's open duffel bag. "Besides, the mission is surrounded by land owned by the US government. And they very much frown on the use of metal detectors on federal property without a permit. They're liable to throw you in the stockade. No joke."

Pete grabbed a pillow from his bed and threw it at Luke. "Very funny."

Luke held up some of Pete's clothes and tossed them over to him. "Here, I picked something out for you. You need to get dressed so we can get going."

Joe grabbed a towel. "Hey, Pete, do you remember seeing one of the Franciscans out last night?"

"One of the Franciscans? You mean when I was walking around?" Pete rubbed his eyes.

"Yeah."

Pete gave a big yawn. "I can't say I did. It's pretty quiet around here at night."

That's strange." Joe scratched his head. "I got up too when I saw you weren't in the room."

"Thanks, pal. It's nice to know you were worried about me."

"I walked around a little and ended up in the chapel, where I found one of the Franciscans. I had a fascinating conversation with him."

"You spoke with one of the friars? I thought they were on a silent retreat?"

Luke stood in the doorway—his arms folded. "Would you two mind getting a move on."

Pete finally lifted himself out of bed. "Maybe they're silent during certain hours of the day."

"I asked if he'd seen you, and he described someone who fits your description walking through the central patio back to the rooms. He also said the person carried something that sounded a lot like your metal detector."

"Well, he might've seen me, but I never saw him."

"So, you're sure you didn't see anybody?

"Not a soul." Pete shuffled across the room, grabbed the handle of the large pitcher on the nearby table, and poured water into the basin beneath it. "You know, I did read something in one of my books about reports of mysterious figures in hooded habits seen walking through the mist late at night—faceless monks roaming the hills surrounding the missions."

"Fine, make a joke about the whole thing. See what I care."

"No, I mean it. They're from pretty credible sources." Pete splashed water on his face.

"It all sounds fascinating"—Luke tapped his watch—"but we need to get going. We're already running late." He threw a towel at Pete. "Dry off, get dressed, and let's get in the car. We'll eat something on the way. Let's go!"

"Wow, look at the height of those towers!" Pete gazed up through the passenger side window of Luke's car. They were driving out of San Francisco on the Golden Gate Bridge.

"You're looking at one of the tallest suspension bridges in the world," Luke said.

"What a view." Joe shifted from one side of the back seat to the other. Luke had told them they'd find plenty to see along the California Pacific Coast Highway. They weren't disappointed. Beautiful beaches, jagged cliffs, giant redwood trees, and the iconic Golden Gate Bridge. Behind them, in the distance, Joe could just make out some of the taller buildings poking out above the mist that blanketed much of the city of San Francisco.

Further along, Luke turned on the car radio. "I'm following any news about the G7 Summit meeting."

"Oh yeah?" Joe angled his head toward Luke from the back seat.

"With Fort Ross so close to San Francisco, especially with the G7 Summit being held there this same week, it's got to be making this year's festival more politically charged than they ever hoped it would be." Luke glanced at Joe through the rearview mirror. "I really worry for the president. He's having to play host to the summit at a time when tensions around the world seem to be reaching a boiling point." He glanced at Joe again. "And I'm sure the Russians have to be one of the president's primary concerns."

As Joe listened to Luke, he suddenly recalled what the old padre had shared with him back at the mission. Though Joe had not given much thought at first to the old padre's words, they all came rushing back to him now. He had spoken of the meeting of world leaders and how the events of this week would be crucial to determining the direction the world may be inclined to go. But he also warned of the world's current dangers and of the presence of powers that were opposed to peace and who were enemies of God and of man.

But what did the words really mean? What was the old padre telling him? Although much of what he said was obscure and difficult to fully understand, Joe did take comfort in the old padre's call for prayer and trust in God's Divine Providence. But he also spoke of how Joe and his friends needed to be especially vigilant and attentive to the events of this week.

Joe mulled over all of these things in his mind. He couldn't imagine how he and his friends would have anything to do with the events occurring at the summit. Sure, they would be seeing the president at the bell-ringing ceremony in a couple of days, but that would be long after the meeting.

"Hey, there's the sign for Fort Ross." Pete pointed through the windshield.

Joe decided he would have to wait until they returned to the mission, where he would hopefully have another chance to see the old padre.

Soon, they pulled into the parking lot, where a long line of people stood. Joe peered through the car window. "I hope they're not all waiting just to get in."

Luke parked the car and turned off the ignition. "I'm guessing it's because of the added security for some visiting VIPs. The Foreign Minister of Russia and their ambassador to the United States were supposed to be coming."

They walked over and took their place at the end of the line. Up ahead, Joe noticed somebody carrying a homemade sign that read, "*Stop Russian Sanctions Now.*" On the other side of the parking lot and well away from the line stood a small group of people holding what had recently become a very familiar sight—the blue and yellow colors of a couple of Ukrainian flags.

"See what I mean?" Luke pointed toward the sign. "Let's just hope nobody wants to cause any trouble, though everybody looks peaceful enough." He shook his head. "It's a shame that it's always the people of warring countries that suffer the most—not the generals or the politicians—regardless of what side you're on."

The plan was to meet up with Father Al at the Fort Ross chapel for the opening liturgy that kicked off the festival, but the line had slowed to a crawl. The wait got Joe thinking again about the old padre he met in the mission chapel the previous night. It had weighed on his mind during the car ride. He recalled what the priest had said about the world's current dangers and the critical nature of the events of that week. What had he meant when he told Joe to look for the signs of God's guiding hand and how he and his friends needed to be vigilant? As much as Joe looked forward to spending the day at the festival, a part of him wanted to get back to the mission. He needed to see the old padre again. He sure hoped he and the friars would still be there when they returned.

He looked at the line of people ahead of them. They'd hardly taken a step in the last few minutes. He took out his phone and decided to do a little research about Fort Ross. Like the missions, the fort was a place of enormous historical significance. During the late eighteenth and early nineteenth centuries, Russia, Great Britain, and Spain were all looking to settle and claim for themselves parts of the Pacific coast of North America. The Russians built Fort Ross to stake their claim in the region.

Over the short time the Russians maintained the fort, it brought together people from the various nationalities and ethnic groups of the old Russian Empire such as Ukrainians, Poles, Belarusians, Russians, Latvians and many others, together with Native Americans from the local tribes, including those from Alaska who traveled to the Fort Ross area to hunt.

"Hey, we're actually moving," Pete said. They followed along until finally making it through the metal detectors and into the interior of the fort.

Joe led the way through the front gate. "What a cool place!"

Situated on a hilly but open plain, the fort commanded a spectacular view of the Pacific Ocean. People wearing bright colors of traditional clothing representing Russian and Native American circulated all around. Displays of arts, crafts, and depictions of early nineteenth-century life dotted the interior grounds of the fort. The mouthwatering aroma of traditional foods and beverages filled the air, something Pete could hardly allow to go unnoticed.

"*Ahh*, do you smell that?" Pete glanced toward the food stations set up nearby. "When do we eat?" The heavenly savor of homemade bread, spicy meats over a fire, and freshly baked desserts enticed everyone's olfactory senses.

Joe tried to keep them moving. "Let's at least find Father Al first."

Joe spotted a large building standing at the far corner of the fort. Its unique structure and rustic appearance resembled something more like a barn. It had what looked like two silos, one behind the other, both sticking out from the roof. As they strode closer, the two silos turned out to be a tower and a smaller cupola, both with a Russian Orthodox cross at the top. Unlike the traditional Western cross, it featured two additional horizontal crossbeams, with one at the head of the cross and the other slanted at the foot. A large church bell hung between two wooden pillars to the left of the entrance. They had found the fort chapel.

A small crowd gathered just outside the chapel door. As the boys approached, the doors opened, and a throng of people began exiting the building. Several Russian Orthodox clergy, all of whom had beards, led the way. Two bishops followed, each wearing colorful embroidered vestments and elaborately jeweled miters—more like a tiara or crown.

Led by the clergy, the crowd formed a procession and began moving along the fence around the interior of the fort. Many of the people carried a variety of religious objects, including beautifully painted icons.

As they passed by, Joe looked back at the chapel door. "Hey, there's Father Al!" Joe began waving as he and the others moved through the crowd, finally catching Father's attention.

"You guys missed the Divine Liturgy," Father said as he greeted the boys.

"Yeah— sorry about that, Father," Luke said. "We had to wait in line for a while." He glanced at both Pete and Joe. "Not to mention, we had a couple of people who wouldn't get up this morning."

"You can't mean these two guys." Father Al grinned.

"It's kind of a long story, Father." Joe felt the need to explain. "I'll have to tell you about it later."

Father turned toward the tall man standing next to him, who wore glasses and appeared to be in his mid-fifties.

"Gentlemen, I'd like you to meet my good friend Father Justin Nowakowski ... but we know him better as Father Nowa—as in *Noah* from the Old Testament." Father Al smiled. "Like me, he's a member of the Congregation of Holy Cross."

"Great to meet you, fellas—Father Sarjinski has told me all about you."

They all shook hands.

"Well, you can't believe *everything* Father Al tells you," Pete said with a crooked grin.

"Don't worry, it's all good," Father Nowa assured them. He took off his ballcap and adjusted the strap, revealing a full head of grayish-white hair that he kept relatively short.

"Father is a professor of history at the University of Portland, a school run by our order." Father Al placed a hand on Father Nowa's shoulder. "He's noted for his study of the history of this region of the country, particularly the Native American people of the Northwest and Pacific Coast."

Luke threw an arm around both Joe and Pete as he stood between them. "Being a history teacher, Father, I think you'll get along just fine with these two guys."

Father Nowa smiled. "I've heard all about the aspiring history scholars within our group." He glanced at Pete. "By the way, that reminds me—congratulations, Pete, on your outstanding accomplishment in the Saint Junipero Serra essay contest. I'd very much like to read it sometime."

"Thanks, Father." Pete took out his phone. "I can send you a copy if you like."

"Sure." They both took out their phones.

"I only wish you guys had gotten here sooner," Father Al said. "You know, our Orthodox brethren really know how to celebrate a beautiful Sacred Liturgy."

Joe nodded his head. "Yeah, we're sorry we missed it too, Father." He turned and watched as the procession continued moving further from the chapel and along the inside wall of the fort. "Where are they going now?"

"It's called a *panikhida*," Father Nowa replied, "which is a requiem prayer service for those who have died. The procession is heading toward the Fort Ross cemetery, where the service will be conducted."

"Who's buried there?" Joe asked.

"The Russians spent a relatively short time here, ultimately abandoning the fort as well the cemetery." Father Nowa stuffed his phone back in his pocket. "Any markers on the graves have since been washed away or lost. But some records exist that list the names of some who died here at Fort Ross. The list includes Russians, American Indians, and persons of mixed blood. Many of the people on that list are probably buried there."

Father Nowa started moving toward the center of the fort where much of the festival activities were going on. The others followed. "That is what I find fascinating when studying and researching the native people of this region of the country. There's an extraordinary history here that I'm sorry to say many in my profession don't always do a good enough job of teaching anymore."

"I guess that shouldn't surprise us," Luke said, "the way education seems to be going these days."

"The Fort Ross Festival begins each year with the celebration of a Russian Orthodox Liturgy in the fort chapel, where we just came from." Father Nowa glanced back at the chapel behind them. "The Russian Orthodox religion is central to the history of this fort. The Russians who originally came to this region brought with them their Christian faith. Russian Orthodox priests who had conducted missionary work among the native Alaskan people did much the same among the indigenous people here in California, many of whom embraced the Orthodox Christian faith and were baptized."

Joe turned his head toward Father Nowa. "That's a story you don't hear much about."

"You're right, but it's a story worth telling. Fort Ross is a remarkable testament to how peoples of various cultures, including Russian and many other European and Asian nationalities and the native peoples of this region, all worked and lived together in relative harmony. Many attribute this genuine cooperation to the Christian values that were taught by the Russian Orthodox clergy who came here. And, as you guys well know, there is a similar story just south of here involving the Spanish missions started by Saint Junipero Serra."

The sounds of singing and music grew louder as they moved closer to the activities of the festival. A large crowd of people circulated among tables and exhibits set up with traditional craft making, games, displays of handmade quilts, wooden sculptures, and many others. A thin cloud of smoke drifted over them from a fire pit, bringing with it a pungent blend of savory spices and seasoning.

The smells could no longer be ignored. "I'm starving!" Pete gazed toward the food vendors. "I say we eat."

Luke looked at Pete. "One of the benefits of learning a language is also experiencing its culture, and especially, its food." Luke put a hand on Pete's shoulder. "I saw someone preparing *blini*, which is sort of like a pancake or a crepe, but better. And *pelmeni*, which is dumplings, and of course, beef *stroganoff* —you know what that is, right?"

"I sure do." Pete rubbed his stomach. "It's one of Mom's specialties back home—and I think I smell some of it right now. What are we waiting for? Let's go!"

Joe turned toward Father Nowa. "Please excuse our friend and his compulsive appetite."

"Are you kidding?" Father Nowa raised his eyebrows, his eyes wide. "You don't think a couple of Polish priests like me and Father Sarjinski can resist an invitation for some good Slavic food, do you?"

"Amen to that, brother!" Father Al chuckled. "I'm getting hungry just listening to you guys. Lead the way, Pete!"

MIRACLE AT THE MISSION

Later that afternoon, the Russian Minister of Foreign Affairs and the Russian Ambassador to the United States visited the festival, as Luke had mentioned. The Foreign Minister took the occasion to speak of what Fort Ross symbolized—a place that once brought Russians and Americans together and still does today. Both he and representatives of the local Kashia Poma people, a federally recognized and active tribe of American Indians, took the opportunity to mark the occasion, now over two hundred years ago, when Russians and the people of the Kashia Poma tribe first met and peacefully negotiated use of the location that would become Fort Ross. "It was a reminder," he said, "of what is still possible today, of Russians and Americans, and all nations of the world, coming together in a spirit of friendship and cooperation."

One of the last and most popular events of the day was a musket and cannon demonstration by members of the Fort Ross militia dressed in their early nineteenth-century uniforms. The roar of cannon fire pierced the air and echoed throughout the surrounding hills. Smoke from the guns drifted across the field toward the crowd where Joe and the others stood watching.

"We probably ought to think about hitting the road soon," Luke suggested as the crowd applauded the final cannon shot. "We've got a long ride back to the mission ahead of us."

It occurred to Joe that they'd been so busy enjoying themselves he had hardly given another thought to the mission and seeing the old padre. It had been a fun day, but they all agreed it was time to start heading back.

Father Nowa invited the group to make a final stop at the chapel where the day had begun. He brought them to the front of the building, where a large church bell hung from a solid wood frame just to the side of the front door.

"Bells have always been important for the life of any community," Father Nowa said as he leaned against one of the legs of the bell stand. "For the Russian and Spanish missionaries, bells called the faithful to worship, announced times of daily prayer, and—being on the frontier—often served as the only liturgical musical instrument." He glanced at the bell. "This was cast in St. Petersburg, Russia, and brought all the way here to Fort Ross." He reached out, touching his hand along the lower edge of the bell. "It's a lasting symbol that reminds us of the people who came here, giving up everything to fulfill Our Lord's call to bring the gospel message to all the nations."

They started making their way toward the front gate of the fort. Pete glanced back toward the chapel. "Isn't the bell that was lost at the Carmel Mission also Russian made, Father?"

"That's right. It was found quite mysteriously after having been lost for many years. It's the same bell we'll be honoring when we attend the event at the Carmel Mission in a couple of days." Father raised his hand and pointed in a direction outside the fort. "Not far from here is Mission San Francisco Solano—the last of the Spanish missions of the twenty-one built in California. Its first bell was a gift given by the Russians from Fort Ross."

As they neared the gate, people around them carried their purchases of traditional hats, candles, straw baskets, and other treasures to put in their cars.

"Hey, I almost forgot," Father Al said as he pulled out his phone. "A room opened up for you guys at the hotel where the conference is, beginning tomorrow night. I put a hold on it for you."

Luke's face lit up. "That's terrific! As much as we've liked the mission, being closer *would* save me the extra drive."

Pete dipped his head. "The mission has been pretty cool." He then looked up. "But being at the hotel might give us a chance to do some other things."

Joe didn't say anything. He thought again about the old padre. He didn't disagree with what Luke and Pete were saying, but he knew he had to get back to the mission. Too many questions remained unanswered that bothered him. But would the monks still be there when they returned? He probably wouldn't be getting back until very late that night. That might be okay, depending on what time they got there. He liked to think there was still a chance he could see the old padre again tonight.

"What do you think, Joe? Is that all right with you?" Father Al asked.

Joe hesitated. From the corner of his eye, he could see Luke staring at him, waiting for his answer. "Whatever you guys wanna do, I'm fine with."

"Very good, fellas." Father began tapping on his phone. "I'll go ahead and let them know."

They passed through the gate and stepped outside the fort. Joe gazed out toward the ocean. The late afternoon sun dipped low along the horizon, a yellow-orange ball with rays of light reflecting toward them along the ocean surface.

"We'll see you guys in the morning at the conference," Father Al said as they made their way to the parking lot. "Our car's over this way."

"Drive safe, fellas," Father Nowa added, "and God bless!"

"You too, Father." Joe smiled and waved. "See you tomorrow."

Pete opened the passenger side door to Luke's car. "Hey, Luke—are we planning on stopping somewhere to get something to eat on the way back?"

Luke glared at him from the other side of the car. "*What*?!" His eyes narrowed as his brow pinched downward. "After what I saw you eat today at the festival?"

Pete pressed his lips together, forming something between a smile and a frown. "Just thought I'd *ask*." He jumped in the car and closed the door.

Fort Ross quickly disappeared behind them as Joe gazed out through the rear window from the back seat. The long drive back to the mission would give him lots of time to think—and worry. Would the old padre still be there when they returned, or would Joe never see him again?

CHAPTER 6

Leo Verenich glanced at his watch. 6:37 p.m. He still had a few minutes to complete the final inspection of the day. As the park ranger responsible for the area around Whalers Cove in the Point Lobos State Reserve, he had to make certain no visitors remained in his sector before the park closed at seven o'clock.

Leo headed down from the museum cabin toward the rocky edge of the water. He had a good view of the portion of the cove to his right, which curved away from him to the north. Two otters frolicked in the shallow surf, a group of mallard ducks quietly moved across the water of the cove, and several cormorant rookeries looked out toward the ocean while resting on the limbs of an old cypress tree above the rocks. He moved along the shoreline between some of the larger rocks to get a better look at the area to the southwest that jutted out into the Pacific Ocean. No kayakers still out on the water to have to remind to come in, which he liked.

His phone vibrated in his shirt pocket. He had received a text earlier that week from his other work, letting him know of a phone call he would be getting about his new assignment. He put the phone to his ear. "Hello?"

"Listen carefully to the following instructions," said a deep, muffled voice with a heavy Russian accent. "You are to secure diving privileges and a launch pass for two individuals and their boat at the facility where you are currently employed." The voice paused. "In addition, you are to pick up a package at the regular harbor location. Details regarding arrival dates for both as well as ship information will be forwarded to you."

Another pause. Leo got the impression that if he had anything to say, he should voice it then. He did admit to not liking being asked to use his primary place of employment for his other work. They had never done that before. But what could the harm be in securing diving and launch passes for a couple of scuba divers—something he did all the time? He decided not to make anything of it. "Understood," he said.

"You will hear from us," the voice went on. "*Do svidaniya.*"

"Goodbye to you too," he said after the caller disconnected.

He shoved the phone back into his pocket and started toward the cabin. He had become increasingly disenchanted with his other line of work. He noticed a change in the way the people there did things—cutting corners, not completely upfront about their business dealings, more secretive about the details of assignments. The latest phone call only added to his concerns.

Nothing he could do about it now. He decided to focus his mind on something more pleasant. His thoughts turned to his childhood home, a little village in the northwest region of Russia. As much as he felt fortunate to be in America, he had his moments when he missed the country of his birth.

After finishing high school, he had worked for the local timber and lumber company. His strong back and sharp wit soon got him promoted to foreman. Unfortunately, with the many downturns in the Russian economy, work in the area dried up, and he eventually found himself without a job.

During this time, the company he had worked for, Usenko Enterprises, approached him with a proposition that would change his life forever. He could still remember the day they invited him down to their office.

"So, Leo," his old boss had said from across his tattered desk, "we're looking to diversify and broaden our business interests, both here in Russia and internationally. We'd like you to consider leaving Russia for the United States. You would live in California. You have heard of it?"

"California? The United States?" Leo struggled to understand. First, they'd let him go due to a lack of work, and now this? An opportunity of a lifetime—to have a chance to go to America, where the streets were paved with gold!

Leo did not have to think about it for long. Nothing compelled him to stay in Russia. Other than some aunts and uncles and a couple of cousins, he had no family to speak of after his parents had died, only a year and a half apart. "Absolutely!" Leo reached across the desk and shook his boss's hand. "Thank you, sir."

Migrating legally from Russia to the United States took a while, but before long, he arrived in California. It was a difficult transition at first. The company arranged for him to live in a rented apartment within a section of the city that had a sizable Russian-speaking community.

Leo walked down to check on the storage units located in the parking lot next to the cove. He alternated between the compartments, making sure the locks were secured on each one. He was thankful for his current job at the reserve, which he enjoyed. He had only worked there for the last five months. Before then, he had worked as a terminal operator at the Port of San Francisco for almost fifteen years—since the time he first had come to the US. He also performed duties for company businesses in and around the greater San Francisco Bay Area, making deliveries, providing transportation for visiting personnel, arranging contacts, and securing accommodations. He had a small group of friends and, although he dated on occasion, marriage never seemed to factor into the equation.

From the storage units, Leo climbed part of the trail that looped around a short slope overlooking where the cove emptied into the Pacific Ocean. He wanted to take one last look to make sure no stray kayakers might still be in the water.

He very much liked the outdoors. After living in San Francisco for many years, he had grown anxious to get out of the city. He had always wanted a place of his own, somewhere with open spaces, and he had saved enough money to be able to do it. In addition, he had hoped to be able to pursue a different line of work, as his job at the docks had taken its toll on his knees.

After not hearing anything for a while, the company finally agreed to his request but let it be known they still wanted the use of his services on a case-by-case basis. No longer required to work at the dockyard also meant not receiving a regular company salary. Fortunately, it did not take him long to land the job at the reserve and find a decent apartment close by.

Not seeing anyone on the water, Leo descended the slope and turned again in the direction of the cabin. It sat in the back end of the cove, beautifully framed by several trees, once considered among the rarest in the world—the Monterey Cypress—now one of the most recognized symbols of California.

He enjoyed explaining the history of the place to visitors. More than a century ago, Chinese, Japanese, Portuguese, and American whalers hunted in that part of the Pacific Ocean near Point Lobos and used the cove as a whaling station. A cabin they built became a museum dedicated to the cultural history of the area. Leo spent a great deal of his time there. Whalers Cove also offered access to some of the finest scuba diving on the California coast.

He reached the cabin and glanced at his watch again: a couple of minutes after seven. He took a final look inside, locked the door, and strolled toward his car. He thought again about his most recent assignment with

Usenko Enterprises. Over the last couple of years, his dealings with the company had diminished considerably. Russia had felt the grip of a declining economy, and with imposed sanctions on, off, and then on again—each one more severe—the Russian people and businesses suffered terribly. The war in Ukraine had made things even worse.

He very much sympathized with the Ukrainian people and could not understand why Russia had taken that action. Perhaps with the change in leadership, things would be different, but he wasn't hopeful. He had seen all this before. He thought back to the collapse of the old Soviet state over thirty years ago with the promise of a new world order and a new Russia. But not much had changed since then. Russia's economy remained that of a third-world country. The only Russians who had benefitted were the oligarchs and those in political power.

Through his work with Usenko, Leo always felt what he was doing somehow helped the people of his home country. Part of him also felt guilty he had been able to come to the United States when plenty of others from the Motherland would never have the chance. But it had been several months since he had met in person with anyone connected with the company. All his dealings now involved emails, texts, or clandestine phone calls. Whenever he completed a job, a deposit would simply be made into his bank account. Lately, his communications with anyone connected with the company could best be described as direct, impersonal, and purely businesslike.

Leo took a day off from work to drive to the Port of San Francisco. He had received a text with the information he needed. Though his visits there had become less frequent, he had made plenty of these runs before. The securing of a "package" normally involved picking up something like a bag, a briefcase, or a piece of luggage and delivering it to someone in the area. He never inquired as to their content, nor did he want to know.

But lately, he had become more curious about what might be in some of the packages and about some of the shadier people he delivered them to. He could only speculate they probably contained money, jewels, or maybe precious metal bullion such as gold and silver, and involved people who preferred not to have such things declared through customs. It was never large enough, though, to think it might be drugs. Leo had always been given assurances he would never be asked to do anything involving drugs. Besides, trying to get illegal narcotics in such small quantities through the port authority with their sophisticated detection equipment and trained dogs simply made it too great a risk. Regardless, he wanted no part of drug trafficking.

"Hey, Leo, long time no see." The guard at the terminal security gate greeted him with a smile.

"Good to see you, Mike." Leo showed him his ID badge hanging from his lanyard. "Just visiting some people. I'll only be a little while."

After parking the car, Leo made his way to the loading terminal at Pier 94 and the manifest office. The digital board there provided the information he needed. It confirmed what he had checked on earlier—the *Encarnación*, a small cargo ship out of Manilla in the Philippines, would arrive on schedule. With trade restrictions placed on Russia due to the recent economic sanctions, alternative means of conducting business had to be utilized. Usenko had to rely on other trading partners with Russia, at least for small jobs like this. Leo could continue to use his familiarity with the port to pick up what he needed and to leave without a problem.

He gazed out a large window that overlooked the harbor. A couple of ships appeared through the mist of a typical San Francisco fog. The ship would take some time to dock, so he decided to get a cup of coffee from the employee lounge.

An hour passed, and after running into some old acquaintances, Leo made his way back to the manifest office and checked the board again. The *Encarnación* had successfully docked, and its cargo was in the process of being inspected and unloaded. He waited a couple of minutes and then headed toward the employee locker room. As he approached, he deliberately slowed his pace, looking at the door. He glanced at his watch. The ship's crew should be coming out any second.

Suddenly, the door opened with people talking and laughing and making their way down the hall. As they passed, Leo casually looked the other way. After waiting at least another full minute, the door opened again. A man emerged. He wore a flat, dark-brown cap and had a toothpick hanging from his lower lip. As he strolled by, he tipped his cap toward Leo and proceeded down the hallway, catching up with the rest of the crew.

Leo waited patiently. He didn't want anyone lingering around once he ventured into the locker room. He opened the door and visited the men's bathroom. After finishing there, he peered around the corner and moved along a hallway constructed of gray-painted cinderblock walls. He found his old locker, something he had been able to retain through some of his connections.

Surprised at how easily he remembered the combination, he opened the locker door without a problem. A large, black carry bag took up most of the space inside the locker. Looking around again, Leo lifted the heavy bag and closed the locker door. He exited the locker room and took the back stairs, which opened to an area of the parking lot outside—an area where security cameras would not see him.

Reaching his car, he shoved the bag into a hidden compartment the company had rigged for him under the backseat. It sure came in handy for jobs like this. He wiped the sweat from the back of his neck with a handkerchief and climbed in behind the wheel. He drove through the parking area and back toward the gate.

The security guards stopped every vehicle before allowing them to go through. Depending on the day and the guard on duty, they sometimes peeked inside through the window of the car, but not much beyond that. Rarely did they conduct full vehicle inspections. Regardless, it always helped to know the security personnel and remain on friendly terms with them.

Drawing nearer to the gate, Leo's pulse quickened. He didn't recognize the guard peering at him from the gatehouse. Where had Mike gone? Leo slowed the car and stopped in front of the gate. To his left, another guard he didn't know got out of the passenger side of a black van parked behind the gatehouse. He had a leash in his hand. The guard stepped aside and out jumped a large German Shepherd. The lettering on the side of the van read *K-9 Drug Detection Services*.

Leo froze. For a split second, he thought about crashing the gate and making a run for it—a crazy notion he immediately dismissed.

The guard stepped from the gatehouse and approached the car. "Good afternoon, sir."

Leo could hardly get his mouth to move in offering a response. "Good afternoon." His voice trembled, barely audible.

"We're going to have to ask you to step out of your vehicle."

Leo heard barking. He looked in the rearview mirror. The other guard walked the dog behind the car, already beginning an inspection. Every bad outcome Leo could conceive of flooded his mind. He had no idea what the bag underneath the backseat contained, and he didn't want to find out, especially here. If the dog found illegal drugs, he knew he faced charges as an accomplice, at a minimum, to a felony, at worst, for trafficking illegal narcotics. That would mean prison time and possible deportation back to Russia.

"Sir." The guard opened Leo's door.

Leo looked down. Sweaty palms gripped the steering wheel. He slowly let go and climbed out of the car. What a way to end his "American Dream." The other guard opened the passenger side rear door and drew the dog near the seat. Leo couldn't bear to watch. He stepped away from the car, closed his eyes, and awaited his fate.

CHAPTER 7

Leo held his breath. A sense of helplessness suddenly overwhelmed him. Finally opening his eyes, he glanced in every direction, desperately seeking an escape option. But even if he made a run for it, he probably wouldn't get far. The guards carried sidearms and wouldn't hesitate to use them on him if he tried. Not to mention the dog would track him down before he got more than a few steps.

"Sir. We're going to have to look inside your trunk."

Leo turned. The guard with the dog had closed the back door on the other side of the car and circled toward the front. "Yes, of course." He followed the other guard to the rear of the car and watched as he opened the trunk.

"What's in the bag?"

Leo always carried a large bag in the trunk with a couple of tools and some old clothes, just in case someone might see him carrying something into the car. "Just some tools and things."

The guard opened the bag and gave it a thorough search.

Leo worried about the dog, who continued sniffing around, pulling on the leash, and moving toward the front of the car.

Finished with the trunk, the guard slammed it shut and swung around toward the driver's side of the car. He stopped and peered into the back seat. "I'm curious ... how's the legroom in the back of these?"

Leo jerked back and blinked a few times, hardly knowing what to say. "Uh ... not bad." He stepped aside as the dog stopped and sniffed his shoes. "But I wouldn't recommend it for people with long legs like yourself ... might be a little cramped." He swallowed hard, trying his best to defuse the tension of the moment.

"You're probably right." The guard glanced again at the back seat. "My wife and I are looking to buy a new car. Not that I plan on sitting in the back much, but you never know."

"Not picking up anything." The guard with the dog tugged on the leash and headed in the direction of the van.

"Looks like you're free to go, sir."

Leo gasped for air, hardly having taken a breath since pulling up to the gate.

"Are you all right, sir? You look a little pale."

"Yes ... I'm fine ... thank you. Didn't have much of a lunch today. Probably just need to eat something." Leo opened the car door and climbed in.

"Thank you for your patience. Have a good rest of your day." The guard pivoted and walked back toward the guardhouse.

Leo turned the key to the ignition, his hand still shaking. He counted the seconds as the arm of the gate slowly rose. He finally passed through, giving a slight wave to the guard. "I'm getting too old for this," he mumbled. Once in the clear, he exhaled a long sigh of relief. He took a final glance in the rearview mirror just to make certain as he made his way out of the port facility and headed home.

Joe yawned as Luke's car pulled into the mission parking lot. He glanced at his phone, 12:14 a.m.

Luke opened the driver's side door and got out. "Get some sleep, you two. We set out for the convention first thing in the morning. Make sure you've packed everything. We'll be staying at the hotel tomorrow."

Pete finally extracted himself from the car and slowly made his way toward their room. Joe had revived himself with a little nap during the trip and planned on making one last stop before turning in. After packing some things in his bag in the room, he looked over at Pete and found him fast asleep. He crept out the door and headed straight to the chapel.

He reached the entrance and pulled on the handle of the large wooden door. He slipped through the opening and entered into complete darkness. And silence. Not even the red sanctuary light burned, nor any of the other votive candles. He waited, hoping his eyes would adjust, but still, he saw nothing. The darkness seemed to envelop him, disorienting him. He felt for his phone, pulled it from his pocket, and turned on the flashlight.

Suddenly, a shadow zipped across his path. Joe lurched backward at the sound of something striking the floor, his heart almost leaped from his chest. What was that? Realizing he had dropped his phone, he reached down at his feet. "Father?" he called out. Getting no reply, he scrambled along the floor, desperately searching for the phone. A waft of air gently touched his face as something moved in front of him. He reeled back and fell awkwardly onto the floor. As he landed, something dug into his lower back. Reaching behind him, he finally felt his phone. He quickly pulled himself up, his hands shaking as he turned on the flashlight again. He shined the light across the empty pews, one empty pew after another. "Father, is that you? Are you there?" Again, nothing. Joe shivered as the chapel suddenly turned strangely cold. Slowly, he began to retreat—his steps, inching almost involuntarily back toward the entrance. He reached behind him, finally feeling the door. Finding the knob, he opened the door and hurried outside.

The night air quickly cleared his head, and he stopped for a moment. He never thought a chapel would be a place where he would feel uncomfortable. Had some small critter gotten in there? The darkness sure made it hard to see anything. Regardless, he couldn't let this distract him from finding the old padre. He circled back to the cloister, hoping to see him there. As he walked along the corridor and turned a corner, he spotted a light flickering from what appeared to be a candle in a window of one of the friars' rooms. Thank God they were still there. Should he knock on the door? What if it wasn't the padre's room? Before he finished his thought, the light went out in the window. Too late to be disturbing anyone now. Not to worry—the monks would rise early for morning prayer. He would have to try to see the old padre then before they left for the convention.

Joe started back in the direction of his room. As he rounded a corner, the sound of howling and shrieking suddenly pierced the quiet of the night. He froze in his tracks. He had been told of coyotes living in the hills surrounding the mission. But this sounded awfully close. He saw the door to his room just ahead and began moving toward it, increasing his pace as he drew closer. A chill shuddered through him as a thickening mist settled around the grounds of the mission. For a moment, he recalled Pete's story about ghostly sightings of faceless monks roaming through the mission grounds late at night. He finally reached his room, slipped inside, then jerked the door shut behind him, making certain to lock it.

Joe threw off his shoes and jumped directly into his bed, pulling the covers up just over the bridge of his nose. He said his prayers as the eerie cries outside gradually receded. Through it all, the rhythmic breathing of Pete enjoying a sound, restful sleep remained undisturbed. Joe marveled. With everything going on that night, Pete, of all people, slept through it like a baby.

For a while, Joe tossed and turned, thinking about the incident in the chapel. He'd read about strange encounters where people were confronted by mysterious phenomena, things not easily explained. What could it have been? Whatever it was, it gave him the creeps. The old padre's face and soothing voice came to his mind. Joe sighed, disappointed he hadn't seen him that night. He would see him in the morning, though. As the peace and stillness of the night returned, Joe's eyes grew heavy, and he soon fell fast asleep.

After arriving at the hotel the next morning, the boys attended Mass in the main convention room, concelebrated by a local diocesan bishop and five other priests attending the conference, including Father Al and Father Nowa. Both Joe and Pete happily agreed to serve as two of the altar servers. After Mass and a nice brunch, The Serra USA Council president kicked off the event, followed by a couple of speakers who discussed the organization's work with young people, particularly in promoting vocations to the priesthood and religious life.

The morning session wrapped up with the recognition of the winners of the Saint Junipero Serra essay contest. Joe smiled at Pete sitting next to him. "Here's your chance to shine in the spotlight, pal." He slapped him on the back. "Just don't forget about your friends after you become famous."

A man on the dais stepped forward and took the microphone. After an introduction, a description of the contest, and the mention of other winners, the speaker finally looked out and announced, "Pete Figueroa from Westthorpe Academy, please come up and be recognized." Beaming a smile, Pete strutted up in front of the entire conference, joining the other winners. After much applause, a few pictures, and a brief interview with a reporter from the local diocesan newspaper, Pete finally returned to his seat.

Joe bowed to Pete in mock reverence. "Way to go, dude, you're a rock star!"

"Yeah, I think I could get used to being a celebrity and living out here." He sat down and leaned back in his chair, a playful grin on his face. "I'm kinda likin' the West Coast lifestyle."

"Sure you do, Petey." Luke rolled his eyes. "But don't you think you oughta finish high school first?"

"Congratulations, Pete. We're all very proud of you." Father Al reached over and showed him his phone. "I got a couple of pictures of you up there to send home."

"Thanks, Father."

Joe glanced all around. "Hey, where's Father Nowa?"

"He had to make some preparations for his talk," Father Al said. "He'll be speaking on a select panel a little later this afternoon. We'll see him then."

A break in the early afternoon offered an opportunity for everyone to mingle, relax, or get something to eat before the next session. Before leaving the mission that morning, Joe had made a quick search of the grounds but couldn't find the monks. He held out hope that maybe they planned to attend the conference. It only made sense that an event like this would attract any number of Franciscans. Joe strolled through the hotel lobby, visiting some of the exhibits, book displays, and other areas of the conference, hoping to find the friars. He inquired with someone at the registration table.

"No, I'm sorry," a very nice lady informed him. "Quite a few Franciscans are attending the event, as you might expect, but none fitting that description."

Joe sighed. "That's okay, thank you." He lowered his head, disappointed. Perhaps he would never see the old padre again, something he had to be willing to accept.

The afternoon involved a breakout session with several smaller talks on a variety of subjects. Joe looked forward to the last event of the day—a combined panel presentation and open forum that included Father Nowakowski and other speakers discussing the legacy of Saint Junipero Serra.

When the time arrived, Joe, Pete, Luke, and Father Al all found seats together near the front of the auditorium as the first speaker was introduced—a college professor of history from Santa Clara University. She adjusted her glasses as she peered up behind her where a map of California appeared on the wide LED screen above the stage. "When the Spanish came to California," she began, "they did so with the intent to befriend the native people with whom they came into contact." She glanced down at an opened portfolio on top of the lectern where she stood. "World history is the story of human beings venturing from one place to another for a host of different reasons. Unfortunately, due to distinctions in culture, language, and interests, history has shown that when two or more dissimilar groups of people come into contact with one another, it is rarely done harmoniously."

She paused. "Long before the Spanish arrived, incidents of disharmony and conflict occurred in many parts of the Americas between various native tribes and nations." The screen changed to a map of Mexico. "The Aztecs, for example, who first migrated from north to central Mexico, subjugated many surrounding native tribes by military conquest, exercised an ethnic superiority over them, and forced hundreds of thousands, including women and children, to be slaughtered by human sacrifice as a blood offering to their deity."

"I remember talking about that in Mr. McAuliffe's history class," Pete whispered to Joe. "The Aztecs would rip a living heart from human victims and offer it to their gods—they kept a record of the number."

Joe nodded. "Yeah, they sometimes killed thousands in a single day." It was an aspect of history Joe had always been curious about. He struggled to understand how some people throughout history could do such things to other human beings.

The speaker paused as the screen switched to a broader map, showing both American continents. "This was a practice done by other groups as well, including the Mayans, the Incas, and Moche civilizations. In North America, although human or even animal sacrifice was not a common practice among native peoples, some did enslave others taken from tribes defeated in battle, utilized torture, upheld ethnic superiority, and even practiced cannibalism."

The moderator of the discussion introduced a second member of the panel. A scholarly figure with a bow tie, he removed his glasses and turned to the audience. "My colleague is exactly right in saying it was never the intention of the Spanish to do away with the native people of the Americas. Unfortunately, what did happen when the two groups came together was something completely unintended—disease."

A picture, comparing many of the various diseases and pandemics that have been known throughout recorded history, appeared on the screen. "The COVID-19 pandemic reminds us of how vulnerable we all are to certain contagions."

Joe thought back to not that long ago when lockdowns, remote learning, and mask requirements were the order of the day. Sadly, he had friends whose relatives had died because of the coronavirus.

"Smallpox and other diseases," the speaker explained, "were responsible for most deaths among native peoples when the Europeans arrived. Unfortunately, there was little known at the time about either how to treat these illnesses or how to prevent their transmission. The native peoples had virtually no immunity to such diseases. However, by the late eighteenth century, a vaccine was discovered for smallpox, and, by order of the King of Spain, inoculations were administered throughout the Spanish Empire, primarily in the Americas, and including California. The vast majority of the thousands who received the vaccination were native people. This is hardly an action one would expect if the Spanish were intent upon genocide."

Joe noticed several hands going up in the audience. A lady from a seat near the back was recognized by the moderator. "Is there any truth," she asked, "to what some would say were practices of coercion, forced conversions, or excessive punishment on the part of the missionaries, even by Junipero Serra himself?" Joe leaned forward in his seat. A question like that deserved an honest and truthful answer.

Another panelist stood up, signaling his interest in answering the question. He was younger, wearing a tan sport jacket, and dressed more casually than the other speakers. "I think the best way to answer that is to look at the man himself." He strode across the stage. "When Father Serra came to California, he wrote of his great love for the native peoples he came to know and serve." The speaker reached into an inside pocket of his jacket, producing a pair of reading spectacles. Placing them on the bridge of his nose, he looked down at some notes he had placed on the lectern. "After meeting some of the native people prior to establishing the Mission of San Diego, his first in Upper California, Serra wrote that, quote, *we were all enamored of them ... these, in particular, have stolen my heart.*"

Not a sound could be heard throughout the auditorium. The words of Father Serra expressing his genuine affection for the native people clearly moved everyone in the audience.

The speaker looked up from his script. "Father Serra founded the missions of California to be places of sanctuary where the friars taught not only the Catholic faith but offered the native people who came to the missions, opportunities to learn techniques of agriculture that would help provide a more stable food supply—something they were not accustomed to as they were primarily hunters and gatherers. The missions also provided protection from enemies, mostly from other native tribes, some of whom were constantly feuding and fighting with one another."

The moderator introduced another panelist—a woman of Native American descent who wore a long contemporary dress with a matching shawl adorned in colorful Indian patterns, and a large ornate necklace of beaded jewelry. "We should also remember there were laws both in Spanish civil law and within the Catholic Church that expressly stated a person can only be validly baptized of their own free will. The missions were built by, for, and maintained by the native people who inhabited them. It is they who have worked these many years to preserve the missions."

She stood up from her chair and stepped toward the lectern.

"It was Father Junipero Serra himself who fought for the proper treatment of the native people. He continually argued that the rights of indigenous people within California should be protected and guaranteed. He presented a thirty-two-point *Bill of Rights* for the Indian people, which was accepted and enacted by the Spanish government. When his close friend Father Luis Jayme was killed by two Native Americans at the Mission San Diego, it was Father Serra who pleaded for leniency for them—that they not be executed by the Spanish authority. Thanks to his efforts, the men were granted a general pardon."

"If I could add to that," offered a voice Joe immediately recognized. Father Nowakowski stood up from his chair. "A man by the name of *Pablo Tac* was born of native parents, both of whom were baptized and lived in the San Luis Rey Mission." Father paused, nudging his glasses above the bridge of his nose. "Pablo himself was baptized as an infant and, as he got older, ultimately decided he wanted to become a Catholic priest. In his writings, he speaks positively about the conversion of his people to the Christian faith and of the good work of the Franciscan missionaries."

"Father Nowa at his best," Father Al whispered. "He's got a real knack for bringing a good and relevant story into the discussion."

Father Nowa lowered his head. "Although Pablo died of an illness before he was able to fulfill his desire to become a missionary priest, his story is but one of the many examples of what Saint Junipero Serra truly meant to the native people of California." Father took a couple of steps toward the middle of the stage. "Today, there are hundreds of thousands of people of Native American descent living in California, many of whom identify themselves as Christian, and a large percentage of those as Catholic." He gazed out over the audience. "It has been the Native American people themselves that have advanced the cause of Father Junipero Serra's canonization and sainthood. During the canonization process, many Native Americans from various tribes were either active or played a direct part in supporting it."

One of the conference organizers appeared on the stage and politely informed everyone that the forum had already extended beyond its allotted time, and he regretted having to bring it to a conclusion. After he thanked the speakers, the audience offered them a warm and spirited round of applause.

Father Al greeted Father Nowa as he stepped down from the dais platform. "Well done, brother!"

Pete raised a hand and gave Father Nowa a high five. "Great job, Father! It's too bad they couldn't give you more time."

Joe joined in the adulation. "You really knocked it out of the park, Father." He glanced at Pete. "Now we've got *two* celebrities to contend with in the group."

They all laughed as they returned to the main floor of the convention. The conference drew to a close with a final prayer and blessing from a Franciscan priest. Joe noted the brown color of the priest's habit—different from the more gray-colored habit worn by the Franciscans who had stayed at the mission with them.

They made their way to the lobby of the hotel as many began saying their goodbyes and preparing to leave. Joe stopped suddenly, having noticed a framed portrait on an easel near the entrance to the convention facility. He stood frozen in place, staring at the picture, unable to take his eyes away from it.

"That is thought to be the only likeness ever done of Junipero Serra," Father Nowa said as he strolled up behind Joe. "Fortunately, two copies were made of the lost original—this is the only one that survived. Well, this is obviously a photocopy of it."

Joe moved closer toward the portrait, studying it. Serra wore a gray habit, his head resting just above the cowl surrounding his neck. Something about his face looked very familiar.

"Interestingly enough, some of the features of Serra in the portrait are probably inaccurate."

"What do you mean, Father?"

"Well, for one, Father Serra is described as having an olive complexion, darker than the portrait suggests." Father Nowa reached out his hand, almost touching the picture. "He is also known to have had brown eyes, not the lighter hazel color like we see here."

As Joe listened, he imagined the picture having the features Father described. His attention suddenly focused on the large crucifix that hung from Serra's neck, a crucifix he had seen before.

"Hey, what's up, guys?" Pete threw an arm around Joe. "I thought you were already outside. Luke says we have time to head over to Point Lobos for some hiking ... maybe even some kayaking or snorkeling."

Joe continued staring at the portrait, hardly acknowledging Pete's presence. "You know, Father, it's not often I see religious orders these days wearing a crucifix that large around their neck."

"Very perceptive, my friend." Father Nowa smiled and nodded, then looked back at the picture. "That is what is called a *Mallorcan* crucifix, one specifically worn by the Franciscan friars who hailed from the Spanish island of Majorca, where Father Serra came from."

Joe stared at the picture again then turned to Pete. "Sorry about that—I promise I'll be right there. Just something I was discussing with Father ... I'll only be a minute."

"All right, but don't be long. We'll be in the car." Pete turned and headed back through the hotel lobby.

"You seem particularly fascinated with the portrait, Joe."

Joe could no longer deny the man in the portrait reminded him of the old padre, though the man in the picture seemed younger. "Yeah, these last few days have gotten me really interested in the whole story of the missions and Father Serra."

"I can certainly understand that. I've been studying these things for many years and never lose my enthusiasm for it."

A small description card rested in the bottom right corner of the frame surrounding the portrait. Joe read the caption. It mentioned how the original portrait was thought to have been painted in 1773. It also provided the years of Serra's birth and death—1713 to 1784. That would make Serra sixty years old when he sat for the portrait and seventy-one when he died. Joe figured the padre he met in the mission church had to be in his early seventies.

"Well, you'd better not keep those guys waiting much longer. They're liable to leave without you. We'll see you when you get back. Enjoy yourselves."

"What's that? ... oh, yeah, thanks." Joe suddenly remembered Pete and Luke outside. "I really appreciate the information, Father. It's been a great help."

As Joe hustled out to Luke's car, he longed to return to the mission, hoping to see the Franciscan friars again—especially the old padre. Somehow, he had to convince Luke and Pete to go back there. But how would he do that? How would he be able to explain all this to them? He had to think of a way.

Pete leaned out the front passenger side window. "It's about time you showed up." Joe opened the back door and climbed in.

Luke started the engine. "Off to Point Lobos." He turned the steering wheel as the car lurched forward and headed out of the parking lot.

CHAPTER 8

Nick Antonovich punched his card through the time clock on the wall in the employee lounge and headed outside to the parking lot. It had been a long day at the golf course.

"See ya tomorrow, Lucky." He waved at Mr. Lucatelli, the assistant superintendent at Pebble Beach Golf Links, who had just pulled up in a golf cart.

"Take care, kid. Bright and early in the morning. Don't be late!"

Nick liked Mr. Lucatelli, who everyone called Lucky. Aside from his occasional gruff exterior, he seemed to have taken Nick under his wing. Nick appreciated that, being the newest member of the grounds crew at one of the most prestigious golf courses in the world. He had his older brother Yuri to thank for landing him the job. They grew up in Encino, California, a neighborhood just outside Los Angeles. They had both worked at a local golf course for a couple of summers—but nothing like Pebble Beach. Their parents had migrated from Russia many years before and settled in Encino, where many Americans of Russian descent resided.

Nick thought back to only a few weeks ago when Yuri visited from his home in Monterey for Nick's high school graduation. The two finally had a moment to talk as Yuri drove them to the small graduation party held at their parents' house.

"How about coming up to Monterey for the summer?" Yuri asked. "I've got a job lined up for you if you want it. You can have your own room—the apartment's got an extra bedroom. Whad'ya say?"

"Really?" Nick jerked his head toward Yuri, his eyes wide. "Do you think Dad would let me go?"

"Come on, you're a high school graduate. You're eighteen years old now, of legal age. You don't need the old man always telling you what to do anymore."

Almost a year had gone by since Yuri had a falling-out with their parents after dropping out of college. He moved out of the house and worked odd jobs until settling in with more steady work. He described it as involving the insurance and finance business. Never quite specific about whom he worked for or where he lived, he informed the family a few weeks in advance that his work required him to move further north to the Monterey area.

The whole situation affected Nick more than he liked to admit. He and Yuri had always been close. He looked up to his older brother and missed having him around. He couldn't bear the thought of boxing up any of the things Yuri still had in the room they shared, hoping someday he would come back home.

Yuri didn't hang around long at their parents' house for the party. He and their father barely spoke. After everyone had gone, Nick approached his parents about Yuri's invitation to visit him in Monterey. Not surprisingly, Nick's father didn't react favorably to the idea.

"But I'll be back in plenty of time to start my classes," Nick tried to assure him. Nick planned on taking classes at the local community college in the fall, something his parents very much supported. His father had always talked about wanting to see his sons get college degrees, something no one in his family had ever done. As a first-generation immigrant from Russia to the United States, he had struggled most of his life trying to make a decent living for his family. But he wanted something better for his boys. Both American citizens by birth, they had the opportunity to get an education and really make something of themselves.

"I'm scared, Nickie, I really am." His father lowered his head, staring at his hands folded in front of him on the kitchen table. Worn and calloused—the hands of a working man—hardened by the toil of labor over a lifetime. He slowly raised his head and looked at Nick. His dark blue eyes were tired and strained. "I'm afraid you'll go up there and not come back. That your brother will talk you into following the same path he has taken."

"That's not going to happen," Nick said, trying to reassure his father. "It's only for a few weeks over the summer. You'll hardly know I'm gone before I'm back again."

"You say that now, and I believe you, son." His father paused. "But you are young, and I know how much you look up to your brother."

"That doesn't mean I'm not my own person." A long silence followed. Nick loved his father and had seen what his disagreement with Yuri had done to him. It had aged and dispirited him, robbing him of his usual strength and vigor. Mom rarely said anything about it, probably not wanting to have to choose sides.

"You are right." His father said, his tone a mix of concession and awareness. "You have fast become an adult yourself ... and I sometimes forget that." He stood up and circled the table, setting his hand on Nick's shoulder. "I guess, in some ways, both your mom and I hoped you would always be our little Nikolai." A smile creased his face, something Nick had not seen very much of lately.

Nick grasped his father's hand. "Maybe my going up to Yuri's might help bring us all together again." Nick stood and hugged his father. All his life, he had known him to be strong, resolute, indestructible—the rock of the family. This moment of vulnerability, a side of him rarely seen, allowed Nick to gain an even greater appreciation of his father. He could feel the hurt in his voice and wanted more than anything to help alleviate the pain. He was convinced more than ever that going to Yuri's would be the right thing to do.

Nick stepped back and looked at his father. "I only want to go with your blessing."

His father lifted his head, his eyes glistening from welled-up tears he could no longer hold back. He smiled. "Just promise ... your mother and I ... that you will come back to us."

Nick hugged his father again. "I will, Pop ... I will."

Not long after Nick got off the bus in Monterey and had settled into the apartment, Yuri arranged for him to interview for a grounds-crew position at Pebble Beach. Securing a job at a place like Pebble Beach required connections, and Yuri apparently had them, establishing some contacts through his work. After only a few days following his interview, Nick was happy to receive a phone call offering him the position.

Though small, Yuri's apartment had two bedrooms and a full bathroom. For Nick, it provided a great opportunity to learn something about independent living—doing his own laundry, preparing meals, and keeping the place reasonably clean.

After a couple of weeks, Nick really didn't see much of his brother. Yuri often worked late, and Nick was up before dawn. Yuri lent Nick his motorcycle for the seven-mile ride to Pebble Beach. It took a while for Nick to get used to the fog that covered the Monterey Peninsula most mornings. He did learn he had to ride a little slower to make sure other drivers saw him.

Though not overly strenuous, his work at the course could be demanding at times. A premier golf course required meticulous care of every inch of ground. His duties included watering, mowing, raking sand bunkers, repairing divots, and working the dew brush and dew whip on the greens in the early morning hours. People paid top dollar to play at Pebble Beach. Reservations were made months in advance, especially during the summer season.

One day after work, Nick returned to the apartment to find Yuri in the kitchen, talking on the phone—a rare early evening when both of them were actually there together.

Nick plopped himself on the sofa, ready to relax after a busy day. He grabbed the PlayStation controller.

"Hey, Nickie, what's goin' on?" Yuri stood at the doorway of the kitchen.

"Not much, stranger. Didn't expect to see you home so soon."

"Unfortunately, I can't stay long. I'm about to head out again." Yuri drained the rest of a Budweiser and tossed the bottle into the recycling bin just inside the kitchen. "But before I go, I did have somethin' I wanted to talk to you about." He strolled into the living room.

Nick put down the controller and turned off the television screen. "Sure. What's up?" Given their work schedules, Nick cherished the few opportunities he had to spend with Yuri.

"How are things at Pebble Beach?"

"Oh, pretty good. Nothing overly exciting. Saw Will Smith there the other day. Not a bad golfer."

"No kidding." Yuri circled from behind the sofa and sat in the recliner across from Nick. "Listen, you remember me telling you how you needed to work hard there and be willing to volunteer for extra hours?"

"Yeah, and I've been doing that. I actually worked some overtime last week. That's a paycheck I'm lookin' forward to seeing."

"Terrific." Yuri glanced at his phone and put it on one of the armrests of the chair. "I've got something to share with you." He paused and looked at Nick. "The company I work for does business with several different clients. One of them involves people who provide information for media outlets. They've recently told us the president of the United States is planning a trip to Pebble Beach to play some golf."

"Yeah, I've been hearing rumors about that at work."

"Exactly—and I can tell you, according to what I've been told, it's more than just idle talk. He's definitely coming." Luke glanced at his phone again. "Anyway, when a president plays golf, the media is rarely allowed access to the course he's on. Some of the people I work for look for ways of working around those kinds of obstacles. They're in the information business and realize the public is interested in knowing something about the president's golf game." He scrunched his eyes a bit as the ends of his mouth turned slightly up. "You know what I mean. They're curious about whether he takes 'mulligans' after a bad shot or whether he kicks the ball out of the rough and into the fairway. They want to know what he wears, who he plays with, and how his overall game is—pretty innocent stuff, but valuable for our client."

Nick nodded his head, giving indication he followed along so far. But he still couldn't understand why Yuri bothered to tell him all this.

"Our client is looking for someone on the inside who would be able to observe the president and provide some of that information to them." Yuri paused. "And I immediately thought of you."

Nick sat silent for a moment, stunned by what he had just heard. "*Me?*" He looked at Yuri, his eyes scrunched tight, thinking this had to be a joke. "But I'm just on the grounds crew!"

"And that's exactly why you'd be perfect for the job. You would only need to make certain you're on the work schedule for that day. After that, it's a simple matter of getting as close to the president as you can and reporting what you see. That's it." Yuri stood, walked to the window, and looked through the blinds. "Oh, and another thing. These people are willing to pay top dollar for that kind of information, which could mean a substantial payoff for both of us."

Yuri's phone buzzed. He picked it up. *"Privet. Da. Podozhdi menya."*

It surprised Nick to hear Yuri speaking in Russian. They spoke it quite often at home, but he hadn't heard it since coming to his brother's place.

"I've got a ride waiting outside." Yuri stuffed the phone into his pocket. "I'm gonna head out for a while. Feel free to use my car if you need it—I'll leave the keys." He threw them on the table. "Do me a favor and think about the offer, okay?" Yuri walked over and put an arm around Nick. They hugged each other. "Don't wait up for me. We'll talk more about it tomorrow. It's important we keep this between you and me—not a word about it to anyone else."

"Okay." Nick got up and walked with Yuri to the door. "Be careful out there." With the late hours his brother often kept, he always worried about him.

"I'll see ya soon." Yuri smiled and gave Nick a wink. He stepped outside and closed the door behind him.

Nick sat back down on the sofa, trying to process everything Yuri had just told him. Up until then, Yuri rarely talked about his work. Now that he had shared something about it, Nick felt a little closer to his brother, which he very much liked. Maybe that's why he hadn't already turned down the offer. He did have to admit, though, that the idea of watching the president *did* make him uneasy. He had come to feel very comfortable at Pebble Beach. He worked hard there like Yuri always reminded him to do, and he got along fine with everyone. He didn't want to do anything to spoil that.

But he also knew having an opportunity to help Yuri with his work might allow them to spend more time together.

Like Yuri said, he really didn't have to do too much other than observe. Maybe it wouldn't be such a bad thing after all.

Over the next couple of days, Nick didn't see Yuri. He would sometimes hear him coming in late at night. Yuri did text him a couple of times, following up about the offer. Nick finally texted him back, letting him know he would do it as a favor to him. Obviously pleased, Yuri told him to keep his ears open at the golf course for anything that might give notice of the president's visit. Nick also had to let the head groundskeeper know he would be available to work as often as possible during the next couple of weeks.

One day after Nick arrived at work, the superintendent asked Nick to meet him in his office right away. Nick headed over immediately. He had never been in the superintendent's office before. He arrived and peeked in through an open door. Mr. Belhumeur sat behind his desk, his sunglasses resting on the brim of his Titleist golf cap. He leafed through some papers while his phone buzzed on top of the desk. "Have a seat, Nick. I'll be right with you."

Nick sat down and glanced around the office. Aside from the usual pictures of the course and other golf memorabilia, he noticed quite an assortment of old license plates and car hubcaps decorating the walls.

Mr. Belhumeur finally looked up. "It's kind of a crazy hobby of mine—hoarding and collecting things." He got up, opened a drawer of his filing cabinet, and stuffed a paper into a folder. "My wife made me move it out of our garage, so I brought it here."

"It looks like a pretty neat collection."

"I'm glad you like it." He got up and walked toward the door. "Nick, I've got a special favor to ask you." He looked out into the hallway, then closed the door. "I'm looking for a couple of guys to be available for a very important assignment next Sunday." He sat back down in his chair. "I wanted to make sure you were available."

"Absolutely, sir." Nick didn't hesitate with his response. "I've let Lucky ... I mean, Mr. Lucateli, know I'd like to work as often as I can."

"Well, I'm glad to hear that, Nick. I always like to see that kind of enthusiasm among our staff."

"Thank you, sir."

"Now, unfortunately, there isn't much more I can tell you about it now, other than we'll need to have you here early." Mr. Belhumeur stood again and circled from behind his desk. "It'll probably require a pretty lengthy shift, with the possibility of overtime pay, of course." He went to the door and opened it. "So, I can count on you for next Sunday?"

"Yes, sir." Nick got up, brushed past Mr. Belhumeur, and stepped through the doorway. "I'll be here for sure."

Mr. Belhumeur reached into his pocket, grabbing his phone to take a call. "Good, Nick. See you then. ... Hello ..." His voice trailed off as the door closed behind him.

If Nick had to bet, the superintendent had just given him notice of when the president would be coming. He needed to tell Yuri as soon as possible. Yuri had warned him not to use electronic devices to relay any information to him about this for fear of detection, so he knew he had to tell him in person.

That evening, Nick stayed up late, waiting for Yuri to come home. He played video games and watched some TV before heading to his room. After reading a little, he struggled to keep his eyes open, but before long, he fell fast asleep. He dreamed of seeing what looked to be the president raising a golf club to hit a shot. Suddenly, he stopped, dropped the club, and looked at Nick, his face contorted, his eyes staring, intense and unblinking, reaching out both hands as if needing help. Secret Service agents closed all around, grabbing and holding Nick. He struggled to free himself.

The sound of a door slamming shut jarred Nick from his slumber. He awoke, disoriented and not sure where he was. In the darkness, he heard footsteps growing louder and coming toward him. “Who’s that?” He sat up in his bed as the door to his room slowly creaked open.

CHAPTER 9

A figure stood silhouetted in the doorway. "You awake?"

Nick sighed, relieved to hear Yuri's voice. "Yeah. You had me scared for a minute."

Yuri took a seat on a desk chair near Nick's bed. "Everything all right?"

Nick rubbed his eyes. "Yeah, just a weird dream, I think."

Nick turned on a side lamp in the room and sat up on the edge of the bed, his eyes blinking as they adjusted to the light. "I wanted to tell you what I heard at work today. I think I know when the president's coming."

"Exactly one week from today," Yuri said, a slight grin creasing his lips.

"How did you know?"

"I've got some reliable sources. And don't forget, some of our clients are counting on that information. Were you able to schedule yourself for that day?"

"Yeah, but ..."

"But *what*?"

"Well, I don't know if I'm feeling so sure about this now." Nick yawned and rubbed his eyes again. He thought about the dream he had but chose not to mention it to Yuri. "I mean, when I first agreed to this, it seemed okay. But now that it's here, and I've had more time to think about it, I'm not so sure."

Yuri stood up and reached his hand toward Nick, placing it on his shoulder. "There's nothing to worry about. We've discussed all this before. All you're doing is keeping your eyes open and reporting on what you see. It's no more complicated than that."

"I know, but what if somebody finds out?"

"Who's going to find out? And even if they did, what's the big deal?"

Yuri stepped back and reached into his pocket. "Remember, I told you how people are willing to pay top dollar for this job?" He looked down at an overstuffed envelope in his hand. "Here's an advance I received today on the payout. We collect the full amount when the job is done." He opened the envelope and ran his thumb along the top of a thick stash of large bills.

Nick looked at it in amazement. He had never seen so much money before.

"There's a lot more where this came from. We can't back out now." Yuri jammed the envelope back into his pocket and sat back down.

Nick sat quietly. Maybe it had something to do with the late hour, or simply being tired, or both. Maybe knowing he needed to be up in a couple of hours to go to work. But for whatever reason, he finally heard himself telling Yuri, "Okay, I'll do it."

"That a boy." Yuri reached over and patted Nick's knee. "I'm proud of you." Yuri stood up. "Now, do me a favor and get some sleep before you have to get up for work."

Nick lay back down on his bed.

Yuri took the sheet and pulled it over him. "Nothing to worry about, you'll see." Nick's eyes were already closed. Yuri turned off the light and quietly shut the door as he left the room.

Nick opened his eyes. He stared into the dark, wondering what he had gotten himself into. He loved his brother and wanted things to be right with him. That he knew for sure, more than anything else. He would do this because Yuri asked him to.

Something still gnawed at him, though. Yuri had assured him it would be easy, with a lot of money involved. But could it be as simple as he made it sound? He rarely ever remembered dreams, but the one he just had left vivid images in his mind. What did it mean? Did dreams like that really foretell some future event? He had heard about such things but hardly thought it would happen to him. He couldn't worry about that now. He closed his eyes again and finally drifted back to sleep.

Nick arrived a little earlier than usual that Sunday morning. He hadn't slept much the night before—his mind racing, thinking about the next day. The president's visit to Pebble Beach had been kept a state secret, at least to the extent that it could be. Most people who worked at the course, or had planned to play there that day, had to know a major celebrity of some kind would be making an appearance. Pebble Beach—considered one of the most iconic and spectacular golf courses in the world, not to mention a place of exceptional natural beauty—attracted the attention of important people from all around the golfing world. Located on the Monterey Peninsula along the Pacific Ocean, it featured some of the most scenic holes in all of golf. It hosted US Open championships, as well as other professional golf tournaments, including the annual Pro-Am Tournament, held every February, where professionals and celebrities played together.

Things did seem different that day, even to those familiar with activities at the course. That morning, lots of people in dark suits and large black sport utility vehicles combed the premises. He heard some of the staff commenting that with the G7 Summit having finished in nearby San Francisco, it had to mean somebody of great importance was coming to play golf at Pebble Beach. Many speculated it would be the president himself.

Nick approached the superintendent's workstation and could see people gathering in front of a metal detector surrounded by Secret Service agents. A couple of people stood in front of him as he waited in line. A sign ahead read, *Please deposit all cell phones*. Anxious and fidgety, Nick's pulse quickened as he felt for his cell phone in the front pocket of his cargo shorts. Once he gave up his phone and stepped beyond the security checkpoint, any thought of changing his mind and trying to contact Yuri would be gone.

"Next." A woman in a navy-blue suit handed Nick a basket and asked him to remove his shoes, keys, belt, any change in his pocket, and, of course, his phone before going through the metal detector. A tall man wearing sunglasses checked to see his driver's license and asked him several questions about how long he had been at the course and a detailed description of the type of work he did there.

"Please turn around." The man proceeded to give Nick a thorough pat-down along with an explosive-trace-detection swab of his hands.

"Nick Antonovich!" A voice called out from behind him as he completed his examination. Nick turned to see the assistant superintendent, Mr. Lucatelli, a couple of feet away.

"Yes, sir?" His voice cracked.

"After you're done here and finished with your usual morning duties, the superintendent wants to see you at the starter's tent before lunch—eleven o'clock. And don't be late."

Nick cleared his throat. "Yes, sir."

"I'm counting on you to do a good job today, kid." Mr. Lucatelli jumped back into his golf cart. "I recommended you for that special assignment, so don't let me down. You'll find out more about it later." He started the motor.

"You're free to go," said another Secret Service agent as he handed Nick the basket with his personal items.

"Thanks, Lucky." Nick watched as the golf cart drove away. After collecting his belongings, Nick found a ticket in the basket with a number and the words "cell phone" next to it.

"Don't lose that," said someone he recognized who worked at the course. "You'll need it if you want your phone back when you leave."

"Thanks. I won't." Nick turned and headed toward the maintenance shed.

Luke's car pulled into the parking lot of Whalers Cove at Point Lobos State Reserve.

"I can't believe it." The news they received from the park ranger at the front gate of the reserve did not appear to sit well with Pete. Kayak rentals had to be obtained at various locations outside the reserve and usually involved a trained instructor guiding a group of kayakers to a specific site. The ranger further explained the rough waters of the ocean breaking against the rocky cliffs there made it hazardous for anyone not familiar with the area and lacking the proper experience.

Joe sensed Pete not wanting to let this go. He had talked about how much he looked forward to doing some kayaking that day.

"But I've done plenty of kayaking at Uncle Rod and Aunt Julie's place in Virginia." Pete opened the front passenger door and climbed out of the car. "It's not like I don't know what I'm doing."

"It's not the same thing, Pete." Luke shut the driver's door and pressed the locking button in his hand. "At Uncle

Rod's, we kayaked on a calm inlet channel, miles from the bigger waters of the Chesapeake Bay. Even then, you had trouble paddling and keeping the kayak straight. This is the Pacific Ocean with waves crashing everywhere."

"I didn't do *that* bad. I finally got the hang of it."

Joe decided he needed to defuse the situation. "Even if we could, we can't rent kayaks from here anyway. I say we hit some of the hiking trails." He unfolded the map they got at the front gate. "Some of the trails here look pretty cool. Look at this one, Pete. It's called Bird Island Trail." He read from the description, "'*A challenging but spectacular coastal hike with sea lions, otters, and harbor seals, small coves of emerald-green water with sea tunnels, caves, and white sand beaches, fascinating rock formations housing tide pools, scenic ocean vistas, views of Bird Island with colonies of birds resting on its rocky cliffs.*' It even says whale sightings are possible depending on the season."

Pete's expression suddenly changed. He raised his eyebrows as he glanced at Joe. "Sea tunnels and caves. I'd almost forgotten. The same ones where the Indians found gold!"

"Yeah, just the kind of exploring and adventure-seeking we've been talking about."

"Well, what are we waiting for? Let's go!" Pete threw on his sunglasses and Westthorpe Academy baseball cap and started for the trail.

"Problem solved." Luke put a hand up and gave Joe a high five as they turned and quickly followed.

Between tours of the Whalers Cove Museum, Leo stepped outside. He peered toward the parking lot adjacent to the cove and saw three young men headed up the sagebrush-covered cliff overlooking the ocean toward the trails. He hadn't seen too many out on the trails today.

"Have a nice afternoon," he said to a couple just leaving the museum.

"You too," the gentleman responded. "And thanks for the tour. We really enjoyed it."

"Glad to hear. Take care."

Leo glanced at his phone. It had taken him a while to get accustomed to the disposable "burner" phone that the Usenko people had given him. They told him everybody had to protect themselves against unwelcomed surveillance and eavesdropping. They also gave him a laptop computer that utilized a proxy server with a virtual private network connection. He had been instructed to destroy and dispose of both immediately upon completion of the assignment.

He'd received no new messages since the phone call earlier that morning. Another voice he did not recognize told him two men towing a boat in a blue pickup truck would be visiting the cove later that afternoon and that he would receive a message of their approximate arrival time. The voice further instructed him to keep the package concealed until he received a confirmation text instructing him to deliver it to one who answered to the name *Adrik Chernov*. This would only happen after they had returned from their trip on the water.

When Leo asked how he would identify Adrik Chernov, the voice merely told him how the name fit his description and Leo would know him when he saw him.

Leo looked out beyond the cove and toward the ocean surf. Did he really need this kind of drama at this stage in his life? He thought about how much he longed to rid himself of these assignments. He made a promise to himself that regardless of the consequences, he would find a way to make that happen.

He glanced at his phone again. It had gotten late into the afternoon, and still no new messages. Like most of his assignments over the years, the waiting always made him the most nervous.

The boys finally reached Bird Island Trail after hiking along some of the interior and tree-covered areas of the reserve. Joe marveled at the stunning views of the ocean as the trail wound closer toward it. Bright orange wildflowers lined their path as birds in the pine trees serenaded them.

Majestic cliffs and large rock formations jutted out toward the sea. Soon they reached the water's edge and looked down from the ridge and onto a strip of white sand surrounded by ocean-carved granite spires.

Joe was happy to see Pete out in front on the trail. He liked to think Pete had forgotten all about kayaking and now had his sights set on some serious hiking and exploring. Pete stopped and pointed down toward the water. "Hey, I think if we keep following this trail, it might lead to a way of getting to the beach down there."

Continuing on, they reached a narrow cut in the rock along the water that offered a spectacular view of a place the map called China Cove, describing it as one of the most scenic locations in the entire reserve. Joe gazed down at an enchanting sight. Emerald green-colored ocean water pooled between jagged rock formations that touched a small white strip of sand. Sea caves and arches cut into rock that stood majestically on each side of the narrow opening.

"Oh, no!" Pete dropped his head. He stood in front of a sign next to some rather crude, narrow steps leading down along the ridge toward the cove below. DO NOT ENTER. CLOSED FOR REPAIRS. A thick strip of orange plastic-mesh fencing blocked the entrance.

"I've got to get down there." Pete peered just over the brow of the cliff. "There's got to be another way down. I'll bet there's a ton of cool things to see in those caves."

Luke rolled his eyes. "Please don't tell me we're going to have that discussion *again*."

Pete didn't respond as he started pacing back and forth, looking down toward the cove.

"I don't know, Pete," Joe said. "Even if someone did find a way down, it's probably tougher getting back up. And probably dangerous." He looked out over the ridge. "That's a pretty steep climb. Besides, it's obvious they don't want anyone going down there."

Luke grabbed the map from Joe's back pocket. "There's plenty more for us to see here." He unfolded it. "This trail leads to another place called 'Hidden Beach.' It's just ahead. Let's go check it out."

They proceeded along the trail, this time with Pete taking up the rear, a good many steps behind. They gained access to two additional beach sites, though neither one was quite as dramatic as China Cove. Weston Beach provided some extraordinary geological features, including fossilized markings on layers of sedimentary rock considered to be millions of years old. Hidden Beach offered a beautiful display of pebbles along the shoreline, each with various shades of colors described on the map as having been caused by the slow cooling of crystallized rock brought up to the surface by volcanic activity over thousands of years. Joe found a pebble he liked and slid it into his pocket. He had hoped Pete would find the location worth exploring, but he spent most of his time moping around, showing little if any interest.

After a while, the boys returned to the trail. They came across a parking lot with a restroom and a small rustic pavilion featuring a variety of displays from around the park. Joe headed to the bathroom with Luke while Pete hung back at the pavilion.

Joe finished first and returned to the pavilion. He looked around but saw no sign of Pete. He decided to double back toward the bathroom, thinking maybe he had gone there. He saw Luke approaching.

"Have you seen Pete? He said he'd be in the pavilion, but he's not there. You didn't see him in the bathroom, did ya?"

"No." Luke stopped in his tracks. "Are you sure he's not just wandering around?"

They both headed back to the pavilion but still couldn't find him. Luke took out his phone. He tried Pete's number, but the call didn't go through. "Must be lousy reception out here."

Joe tried his phone. "Same problem here." He surveyed the area around them, trying to figure out where Pete might have gone. "You don't suppose he headed back to China Cove, do you?"

"And do a harebrained thing like climb down that cliff?"

They both looked at each other. Luke glanced down the trail, then back toward Joe. "I'll head back to the cove. You stay here in case he just wandered off somewhere and comes back." He looked at his phone. "Give me about fifteen minutes before trying to call me. If we can't connect, just follow me down to the cove."

"Will do. Good luck." Luke started back on the trail. Joe watched him as he hurried down the slope and disappeared behind a cloud of dust.

CHAPTER 10

Nick swallowed the last bite of his turkey sub and washed it down with what was left of an Arnold Palmer iced tea lemonade. News spread the president would be arriving at Pebble Beach sometime in the afternoon. That explained why lunch had been brought out to the members of the groundskeeping crew—wanting to restrict movement around the course.

His stomach tightened. As much as he had arrived that morning knowing the president would probably be there, the certainty of it finally sunk in. Just before lunch, the superintendent told Nick and a couple of other guys from the crew that they would be working with the president's playing group, raking sand traps, locating balls after errant shots, replacing and repairing divots, and fixing spike marks on the greens. That should put him close enough to get the information he needed. Still, the most closely guarded human being on the planet would have Secret Service personnel all around, watching every move the president made. What if one of the agents suspected something and started asking Nick questions? What if he cracked and told them everything? Could he be charged for spying on the president of the United States?

Whenever he had brought these things up with Yuri, Yuri always assured him he had nothing to worry about. As much as he wished he could back out, he didn't want to disappoint his big brother ... or his father, for that matter, who had finally given his approval for Nick to visit Yuri for the summer. He had convinced his father that visiting his older brother might be a good thing for the family. To that end, Nick realized that coming to see Yuri should involve helping heal family differences, not creating new ones. He took a deep breath and forced the thoughts from his mind. No more analyzing this. He would simply have to do it.

Tossing his empty drink bottle into a recycling bin near the entrance to the tent, Nick stepped outside and headed toward the outer maintenance facility located between the sixth, eighth, and fourteenth fairways. The sun shone brightly in a clear blue sky, making him wish he could enjoy the day in a much more relaxed way.

After reaching the facility, he crept in between two of the supply sheds, turning his head from side to side. Not seeing anyone, he opened one of the sheds and slipped through the door. The only light inside came from two small windows and a skylight in the roof. He listened for any sound outside as he crept toward one of the rear compartments where a stack of thick water hoses rested in the corner. His pulse raced as he crouched down and guided his right hand along one of the hoses near the bottom. He felt the large nozzle and pulled it toward the front, moving the whole pile with it. Suddenly, a golf cart came whirling into the maintenance yard just outside. Nick stopped and listened.

"Are you in here, Antonovich?"

Although somewhat muffled, Nick recognized the voice immediately. He quickly unscrewed the nozzle and reached into the mouth of the hose. A drop of perspiration beaded on his forehead. With a sweaty palm, he struggled to loosen a strip of duct tape inside the hose. Finally, with one hard pull, the tape came loose, and with it a phone. Although he had never been comfortable with the idea of stashing one there, Yuri convinced him that a burner phone, even if someone found it, could never be traced to anyone.

The sound of footsteps drew nearer, stopping just outside the shed. Nick flinched, causing something to drop, hitting his foot and landing on the floor—the phone. In one fell swoop, he bent down, picked it up, and grabbed one of the hoses, just as the shed door swung open.

"What's going on in here, Antonovich?" Mr. Lucatelli stood at the door entrance, glaring at Nick. "And what are you doing using those old hoses? You know we don't use those anymore."

Nick forced a smile. "Sorry, sir—I guess I forgot."

"You forgot, ugh." Mr. Lucatelli traipsed across the floor to the other side of the shed, shaking his head. Nick quickly slipped the phone into his pants pocket.

"Here, this is the hose you want." He grabbed it and tossed it toward Nick, where it landed on the floor near his feet.

"Thanks, Lucky." He lifted the hose and threw it over his shoulder.

"You can thank me by getting your slow-moving rear-end back to work." Mr. Lucatelli turned toward the door. "The watering's not gonna get done by itself."

"No, sir ... I mean ... yes, sir." Nick followed Mr. Lucatelli out the door.

"You think you can have it done before the president gets here?"

"Absolutely, sir."

Nick moved toward one of the small utility vehicles and tossed the hose in the back.

"Good, because the superintendent wanted me to check to see if you could stay a little later this afternoon. It's looking like the president might be delayed a bit in getting here."

"I can stay as long as you need me. Not a problem."

"But don't think for a minute this gives you all day to get the watering done." Mr. Lucatelli jumped back into his golf cart. "And as soon as you're finished with the watering, meet me up at the ninth tee box. I've got something else for you to do there."

"Yes, sir." Nick climbed into the utility vehicle, started the motor, and headed out of the maintenance yard. The cool breeze rushed through the open cab and across his face—a much-needed relief from his near disaster in the shed. He felt for the phone, still secure in his pocket.

When he arrived at the twelfth hole, he pulled into an area of trees and bushes adjacent to the green, where he couldn't be seen. He turned and surveyed the grounds behind him, having reached the farthest extension of the golf course on the south end. The president wouldn't be playing this side of the course, which meant no Secret Service agents to worry about up this way. Just the same, he looked around before reaching into his pocket.

He checked the phone—still no message. Yuri told him to expect a text with instructions sometime before the president's arrival.

Nick jumped out of the utility vehicle, suddenly remembering what Lucky had told him. He grabbed the hose out of the back and carried it down the twelfth fairway a few yards. After locating the underground pipe head, he connected it to the end of the hose and began watering a couple of areas that had been previously marked. As much as the course utilized an automated sprinkler system, a few areas here and there always required some additional watering.

After doing the same thing on fairways ten and eleven, he returned to the utility vehicle and prepared to drive back across the course to follow up with Lucky at the ninth tee. He took a quick glance at his phone again. A message had finally arrived.

GIVE FULL DESCRIPTION OF PREZ CLOTHES ASAP. NOTIFY WHEN PREZ NEARS HOLE #7. TEXT Y TO CONFIRM.

Nick stared at the message. He read it again. The instructions seemed simple enough but awfully strange. He could understand the interest in what the president might be wearing, but why the attention to the seventh hole? Unfortunately, he didn't have time to think about it. He had to go meet Lucky. He typed in "Y" and sent the message.

Nick approached the ninth tee and pulled up next to Mr. Lucatelli, who sat in his golf cart, his arms folded across the steering wheel. "Hey, kid—time to saddle up. The president should be here any minute. I want you to get up to the first tee right away. Look for the superintendent."

"Yes, sir." Nick immediately turned the wheel and started heading up the cart path.

"Good luck, kid. And don't screw up."

Nick looked back with a grin and waved. A mixture of both excitement and nervousness suddenly struck him. The time had arrived. He couldn't turn back now. Soon he would be in the company of the president of the United States. He only wished he could feel happy about it.

The president's limousine pulled up to the front of Pebble Beach Golf Course with a full escort of California Highway Patrol police troopers on motorcycles and numerous Secret Service vehicles.

A blue pickup truck with a boat and trailer hitched to it sat idling on the side of Seventeen Mile Drive, a short distance from the entrance to Pebble Beach Golf Links. After the last vehicle of the president's motorcade completed the turn into the course, the truck merged back onto the road and headed south.

A man in the passenger seat of the truck touched a number on his phone and brought the phone to his ear. "Yes. Fifteen minutes," he said with a Russian accent.

"Message received," Leo Verenik answered on the other end. He jammed the phone back into his breast pocket. The mysterious Adrik Chernov would soon be there. Leo thought back to what his contact had told him about Chernov's name fitting his description. He never cared much for riddles, but this one did have him curious. He gazed out over Whalers Cove and sighed. Everything seemed quiet and peaceful— maybe too much so.

Luke finally reached China Cove and stood where they had been just over an hour ago. He peered down over the ridge and onto the small beach below. Two harbor seals played in the shallow water while another sunned itself on the white sand—but no sign of Pete. He pulled out his phone and tried Pete's number again. It rang a couple of times but suddenly lost the signal. "Pete, are you down there?" His voice echoed, followed only by the sound of seagulls and the ocean waves crashing against the outer rocks.

It was getting late, and the reserve would probably be closing soon. With no one else around, he began to worry. He had no phone reception and couldn't know whether or not Pete may have returned to the pavilion with Joe.

Luke scrambled along the ridge, trying to find another way down. Frustrated, he followed the trail as it semicircled around the cove, hoping to be able to gain a better vantage point. If Pete somehow got down there, Luke had to find out. God help us if he had fallen and gotten hurt.

"Pete!" he called out again. Still no answer. He glanced at his phone. No one had tried calling him, as far as he could tell. But even if they had, the signal remained weak. Going back and getting help seemed the only thing to do. He remembered seeing a park ranger in the gray cabin they passed when they first pulled into the reserve.

Luke scampered back up the trail and headed toward the pavilion. Before long, he reached the parking lot again, where Joe stood speaking with an older man and woman both decked out in hiking apparel and carrying walking sticks. Seeing Luke, Joe nodded toward the couple then came out to meet him. "Any luck?"

Luke shook his head as he caught his breath. "Nothing."

"Same here." Joe glanced back behind him. "The couple I just talked to told me phone reception is pretty lousy out here."

"No kidding."

"They also said we'd be lucky to see a park ranger in this section of the reserve, especially this late in the day." Joe pointed toward the pavilion. "There's an emergency phone up there, but it doesn't work."

Luke glanced at his phone. "The first thing I'm going to do when we find that kid is slap him upside the head. Then I'll give him a big hug and tell him how much I love him."

"Don't worry, we'll find him."

"It looks like the only choice we have is to head back toward Whalers Cove and find that ranger I saw in the gray cabin."

"I think you're right."

Luke reached into his backpack, pulling out a notepad and pen. He wrote a brief note to Pete.

Meet us at Whalers Cove. Call me if you can.

He poked the note around a nail head jutting from the frame of the pavilion. If Pete walked up that way, he couldn't miss it. He and Joe got back on the trail and headed toward Whalers Cove, going as fast as their legs would take them.

Nick scampered down the first fairway well ahead of the president's group. He and another member of the grounds crew on the other side of the fairway went out ahead to make sure no problems arose on the fairways, bunkers, or greens.

Any errant shots into the rough or beyond, especially off the tee, would require them to be spotting the balls. Due to the late start, Nick was told the president's group would play only nine holes, going from the first hole through the seventh and then doubling back to finish out the round with holes seventeen and eighteen. Nick thought back to the text message he had received earlier. With the seventh hole still in play, it would be good news for the people who wanted to know when the president approached that hole.

Earlier, Nick had gotten close enough to get a description of the president. He looked to be just above average height—maybe about six feet tall. He wore a black San Francisco Giants cap with orange lettering in the front and an orange bill—the team's colors. He had on dark gray pants and lighter-gray golf shoes with a maroon-colored long-sleeve top. Nick ducked into one of the portable bathrooms on the course and sent a text with the information. He immediately received back,

> **INFO. RCVD. NOTIFY WHEN PREZ APPROACHES HOLE #7.**

After reaching an area a little more than two hundred yards from the tee, he turned around to see the group preparing to hit. It looked like the president would be the first after placing his ball on the tee and taking a few practice swings.

As he waited, Nick thought again about the seventh hole and the repeated message he received. Why the interest in that hole? No doubt, it was one of the most celebrated and picturesque holes in all of golf. The hole was a short par three by most golf standards, only a little more than a hundred yards in length. It played downhill with about a forty-foot drop from tee to green. But the green was located on a small peninsula that jutted out into the Pacific Ocean with waves crashing high against its rocks. Sand bunkers surrounded the green, mixed with patches of tall, thick grass. The view the players had when they looked down at the hole was both spectacular and intimidating.

At the first tee, the president raised his club and hit a decent shot that came to rest in the light rough on the other side of the fairway. As he waited for the other players to hit, Nick continued to rack his brain. Could someone else be watching who was also interested in the seventh hole? If so, who ... and why? He became more uncomfortable the more he thought about it. For now, he would have to keep his eyes wide open for anything that might give him a clue.

Nick headed toward the first green as the players prepared to hit their next shot. With every step he took, the seventh hole loomed closer. He had to find out why somebody would want to know when the president would be there. And he would have to do it quickly.

Captain Kevin Holmes of the US Coast Guard commanded the USCGC *Claude S. Morgan*, a 154-foot Sentinel Class, Fast Response Cutter Patrol Boat, designated for temporary duty off the Monterey Peninsula. He and his crew patrolled the waters within a two-mile radius of the shore near Pebble Beach Golf Links on a day when the president of the United States would be visiting the course. Alerts had gone out that all recreational and boating activities would be suspended within that area throughout the day.

Normally, the waters surrounding the Monterey Peninsula would be filled with people doing all kinds of activities like boating, sailing, fishing, whale watching, glass-bottom boat tours, surfing, scuba diving, and kayaking. Not to mention the many people who simply enjoyed spending time on the beach in the area just below the golf course.

The captain stood on the bridge, peering through his binoculars, scanning the expanse of ocean between ship and shoreline. Up to that point, the day had gone rather smoothly, although he didn't particularly like the news of the president's late arrival to the course. The longer he had to enforce the restricted area, the more likely somebody would violate it.

Protocols like these were standard procedure for such assignments. The establishment of a perimeter surrounding a two-mile radius was considered an acceptable distance in order to minimize the possible threat of a long-range sniper attack or similar dangers.

And as if the captain didn't have enough to worry about, a group of whales had already come dangerously close to the ship. Monterey was a popular stop for these large migrating sea mammals. They visited there throughout most of the year to feed on the rich supply of plankton, krill, anchovies, and sardines found in the waters offshore. Having reached levels of extinction after years of whale hunting, they began to increase in number again and no longer felt threatened by boats they encountered in the water. Some of them had been known to become quite friendly, sometimes swimming alongside boats and even touching them.

This was something that might be welcomed by whale-watching boat tours, but not by a Coast Guard patrol ship trying to do its job. Though the whales themselves were usually found farther out to sea, sometimes they followed the ridge along the underwater canyon that Monterey was famous for and ventured closer to shore in search of food. Today happened to be one of those occasions, much to the captain's dismay.

"How do you convince a whale not to swim within a restricted area?" Captain Holmes asked his executive officer.

"Not something I would even try, sir."

The captain lifted his binoculars again and trained them toward the shore. Small patches of white sand bunkers dotting the landscape stood out among the finely manicured greens and fairways of the golf course. At least for the moment, no one appeared to be in the area of the course along the coastline where the president would be playing. "Hopefully, it's only for a short time, but I've got no other choice." He put down the binoculars. "Tell the helmsman to direct us out of this sector and further out to sea until we know for sure we're not about to butt heads with a humpback."

"Aye, aye, sir." Within seconds, the ship began to turn, heading out into deeper water and further away from the shore.

"Contact command and let 'em know we've been forced out of the restricted zone at least temporarily." The captain turned and looked out over the side of the ship. A whale spewed water from its blowhole, not far from them. "And for heaven's sake, keep an eye on those whales so we can get back to where we need to be!"

CHAPTER 11

Leo gazed out the window of the Whalers Cove cabin. A blue pickup truck towing a boat eased into the parking lot and stopped next to the boat launch. Tinted glass windows prevented him from seeing inside. More than a minute elapsed before the driver's door swung open and a man emerged wearing a black wetsuit, sunglasses, and a black ball cap with the bill turned to the back. Leo opened the door to the cabin, stepped outside, and started toward the parking lot.

As Leo approached, the man from the truck walked very slowly as if expecting Leo to come to him. He was just above average height with a cigarette dangling from his lower lip. He took off his cap and ran his hand through a straggly mop of brown hair with flecks of gray that fell over his eyes but close-cropped along the back and sides. He stopped at the edge of the parking lot.

Leo met him there. "Good afternoon."

The man said nothing as he looked down at Leo's name badge. He took a drag from his cigarette and exhaled a cloud of smoke.

As the offensive odor reached Leo's face, he turned his head and pointed to a nearby sign along the path that read, NO SMOKING.

The man glanced at the sign. "Huh." Returning his gaze to Leo, he took another drag from the cigarette, flicked the butt to the ground, and crushed it under his boot.

Over the years, Leo had met all types in his work with the company. Some he merely learned to tolerate. He waved his hand through another cloud of smoke. "What can I do for you?"

The man reached into his pocket and pulled out a piece of paper—a day pass covering boat launch and diving privileges for two people.

Leo lifted his clipboard to check the log sheet. The invoice number matched the one on the paper—the same one he had arranged days ago.

"You've got a good day to dive, though it's getting a bit late." Leo handed the pass back to the man. "You're the last group out, so you shouldn't have anybody else in your way." Leo shielded his eyes and peered out toward the ocean. "Incidentally, be aware the Coast Guard is maintaining a restricted area a couple of miles up to the north—something going on at Pebble Beach, I think. It shouldn't affect you as long as you're on this side of the dive site." Leo glanced back. "Oh, and tell your friend I've got your package waiting for you when you return."

The man looked in the direction of the cabin. "*Goowd.*" Without another word, he turned and began walking back toward the truck. The passenger door suddenly swung open, and a man with shoulder-length black hair and a thin black beard got out. His black tank top revealed swirling tattoos mostly done in black ink covering every inch of his arms. Though a sprinkling of gray in his beard suggested he was older, he had a muscular frame and was taller than the other man. He stood and glared at Leo with penetrating dark eyes, his thin brows drawn together below a creased forehead. His grim expression gave way to a brief turning up of one corner of his mouth as if to acknowledge Leo.

After exchanging words with the other man, he tugged a long black bag from the cab of his truck and slammed the door. Walking with a purposeful stride, he carried the bag to the boat and set it carefully on the deck. He put on a wetsuit as the other man got back in the truck and began backing the boat into the launch area along the shoreline.

On all previous assignments, Leo had kept his distance from the contacts while simply carrying out his instructions. Although this assignment had been different—especially the way it involved his work (something he didn't particularly like)—he didn't need to make any further efforts to converse with these men. His primary contact had been quite accurate in saying how Chernov's name (which means *black* in Russian) would fit his description. Even the name Adrik had a meaning associated with the word *dark*.

As the men prepared to launch the boat, Leo made himself busy checking some of the equipment sheds adjacent to the parking lot. Within a couple of minutes, the boat engine roared, carrying the two men toward the mouth of the cove and into open water. Leo strolled to where they had parked the truck and the boat trailer. Oddly, the men had disconnected the trailer from the truck and had backed the truck into a parking space as if prepared to make a hasty exit upon their return. What did they plan on doing with the boat—leave it in the cove? That wouldn't go over well with his supervisor.

And going out this late for a scuba dive? Everyone knew the best time to dive happened between midmorning and midafternoon, when the highest angle of daylight penetrated the water to better see beneath the surface.

Leo returned to the cabin, where he decided to do some research. He typed the name Adrik Chernov into his laptop. Finding little of what might be called reliable information, an obscure website revealed an article about suspected private paramilitary contracting operations within Russia. A short paragraph mentioned a couple of names, including Adrik Morozova, also thought to be known as Adrik Chernov. A brief bio revealed Chernov had served in the Special Operations Forces of the Russian Federation and later as a highly skilled sniper in an elite unit specializing in counterterrorism, countersabotage, counterintelligence, and high-value targeted assassinations and retaliation strikes.

The article explained how, after seeing action in Chechnya, Crimea, and Syria, nothing much was known of him other than speculation about his involvement in secretive paramilitary nonauthorized missions in close cooperation with the Russian military, a practice officially considered to be illegal in Russia. Although he was currently assumed to be retired from active duty in the military, the article further suggested Chernov may have hired himself out as a private contractor with ties to organized crime syndicates, including *Bratva*, the Russian mafia. The article also mentioned him as a person of interest in the murder of at least two private Russian citizens.

Leo sighed and put his head down. Maybe he had held on too long to his work with Usenko. Times were passing him by faster than he wanted to admit. Although he had never been naïve enough to think that some of the jobs he had been assigned could be considered *above board*, he had always been able to put such thoughts in the back of his mind. He had convinced himself that, regardless of the circumstances, the work he did went toward helping his home country. But lately, he had grown more suspicious and concerned about what some of these assignments really involved and whether he could be implicated if something went wrong.

Why would someone like Adrik Chernov be here in Monterey, California? After receiving the assignment, Leo had been told of its importance and how it might help bring about some economic relief for Russia. But the idea of Adrik Chernov being involved—Leo shook his head, tension knotting his insides. A professional assassin had to be here for more than just scuba diving. And on top of that, Leo had been instructed to give him the bag he had picked up in San Francisco after his return in the boat. Whatever Chernov planned on doing, Leo would be directly tied to it.

A profound gloom seized him. If Chernov planned to harm someone, that would make Leo an accomplice to a capital crime or, at the very least, an accessory. He glanced at the computer screen again, hoping to discover something that might dismiss the possibility of such an alarming scenario. Chernov's name appeared again in the article, this time with a hyperlink connected to it. Clicking it took him to another article, one with a picture too small to make out. He hesitated before bringing the cursor over to enlarge the picture. As he pushed the button on the mouse and stared at the screen, a tightness gripped his chest.

The dark eyes and features of the man in black from the parking lot matched those of the man looking at him from the computer screen. Though he appeared younger in the picture and wore a Russian military uniform, Leo was sure it was the same man he had seen moments before.

Leo slammed shut the computer screen, his mind racing. What had he gotten himself into? He stood and peered out the side window of the cabin. Suddenly, he remembered how he had informed Chernov's friend about the boat restriction bulletin that had gone out earlier that day. He opened the computer again. With Pebble Beach so close to the reserve and a place that attracted all kinds of celebrities and dignitaries, bulletins like these occurred often enough.

Could that be what had brought Chernov here? Leo glanced down at the screen. A news item on his web portal caught his eye. The G7 Summit in San Francisco had ended earlier that day and without Russia's involvement. A subtext mentioned something about what the various world leaders who had participated in the summit would be doing before returning home. He clicked on the link and read further. After the summit, the president of the United States had planned to visit the Carmel Mission for an event there. But before that, the president would be stopping by Pebble Beach for a round of golf that very afternoon.

Leo sat frozen. Is that why Chernov was here? He could hardly comprehend the thought that Chernov planned to harm the president of the United States. How could such a thing be possible? But the more he thought about it, the more everything seemed to convince him it was true. Unable to move, his mind returned to some of the things he had been asked to do over the years—things he knew were highly suspicious but chose to say nothing about. Had he grown so accustomed to turning a blind eye that he could allow something like *this* to happen? He knew the time had finally come for him to take a stand. He had to think of a way to stop this and stop it quickly. But how, and would it be too late?

Luke hustled down the paved trail that overlooked the ocean. At the top of the hill, he'd glimpsed a small boat leaving Whalers Cove, but his focus now turned to the cabin near the parking lot below.

"Think anyone's in there?" Joe asked, coming up alongside Luke.

"That's what I'm hoping. *Somebody's* got to be around to help us find Pete."

They rushed toward the cabin, finally reaching the front door. The building looked more like a rickety old shack that had survived from the whaling days of a century ago. The grounds surrounding the cabin displayed an assortment of artifacts that included old whale bones, several large tusks, a whale skull, and a large, rusted ship's anchor, which was chained to one of the surrounding gray cypress tree trunks. Paned glass windows flanked the front door. A sign made of whalebone, with the words *Whalers Cabin Museum*, hung on the wall to the left of the entrance.

Anxiety growing inside him, Luke stepped through the cabin doorway first. A harpoon hung on one wall, a huge map next to it. More pictures and large-bladed instruments adorned other walls. The life-sized wax figure of a man dressed in an old-fashioned deep-water diving suit stood stationary in one of the corners.

"What can I do for you, fellas?" The park ranger they had only seen a glimpse of earlier stepped out from a back room. The name "Leo Verenich" appeared on his name tag.

"Boy, are we happy to see you." Luke threw his hands up, relieved that they had finally found someone to help them. "It's about my brother, Pete."

"What seems to be the trouble?"

With his training in the Russian language, Luke could detect a slight Russian accent in the park ranger's voice. "We were hiking on the other side of the reserve but then stopped to take a break." Luke paused, glancing at his phone for any new messages. Still nothing. "Both Joe and I went to the bathroom, and when we came out, my brother Pete was gone. So, I doubled back toward China Cove while Joe stayed where we were, but there was no trace of him."

The park ranger nodded. "How old is your brother?"

"He's sixteen."

He moved toward a countertop near the back of the room. "You mentioned China Cove."

"Yeah. He seemed fascinated with the place after we saw it. He got upset when the steps leading down to it were off-limits. That's why I doubled back, thinking he might have gone down there."

The ranger grabbed a map, opened it on the countertop, and asked the boys to show him exactly where they had been on the reserve and where they had last seen Pete. After getting a full description and other information, he took the radio from his belt and made a call. He put the receiver down. "We've got a number of our personnel looking for him right now, including somebody climbing down to the beach at China Cove." He folded the map back up. "Don't worry, it's not the first time someone here has gone wandering off only to turn up safe-and-sound."

"That's good to hear." Luke sighed and leaned against the counter, suddenly realizing how drained he felt.

"We'll find him." Joe put a hand on Luke's shoulder. "Let's keep the prayers going."

"Now, if you'll excuse me, I've got another call to follow up on." The ranger grabbed a holster with a gun strapped in it and buckled it around his waist. "I suggest you stay here and make yourselves comfortable." He gave Luke a business card with a phone number on it. "You can use the landline phone here in the back of the room if you need to reach me. Just ask for Leo. Either I or someone else will be in touch as soon as we know something." He swung around and quickly dashed out the cabin door, heading toward the cove.

Nick strode from the fifth-hole green to the sixth-hole tee box. He gazed out across the fairway. Like many of the celebrated holes at Pebble Beach Golf Links, the sixth hole offered its share of unique challenges. A long par-five, over five hundred yards in length, a player's tee shot had to avoid fairway bunkers to the left and the so-called *Cliffs of Doom* to the right where a stray shot could easily end up in the ocean. An approach shot from the fairway to the green required hitting over a high ridge on the other side of the same cliff and onto a rather small and undulating green hidden from view, guarded by bunkers on both sides.

The president's group had been playing slowly, thanks to an assortment of stray shots. The sun had already dipped behind some clouds that had settled along the ocean's horizon as early evening approached. When the president's group finally began moving toward the sixth tee, Nick headed down the fairway to position himself for the next round of shots.

Suddenly, he realized any opportunity he would have to relay the president's approach toward the seventh hole would have to happen soon. The greens for both the sixth and seventh holes jutted out along the furthest extent of the peninsula, right out into the Pacific Ocean. Completely exposed, this area of the golf course lacked trees or anything else that could provide cover. Once out there, Nick would have no way of using his phone without being noticed.

He had to act fast. Walking along the left side of the fairway, he glanced behind him and noticed the president's group had not quite reached the next tee. He turned and peered down the fairway where he could see a few Secret Service agents scattered across the course a good distance ahead of him. He quickened his pace and subtly angled his steps in a way that would allow him to move closer to the outer-course maintenance facility just to the left of the fairway bunkers and the cart path. The only opportunity he had to use his phone would be there and out of sight.

He ducked behind one of the sheds. Looking from side to side to make sure no one had seen him—Nick directed his steps toward one of the portable bathrooms. Once inside, he took out his phone and hurriedly began texting.

NICK: FORCED TO SEND MSG NOW. PREZ ON #6 TEE. SOON ON #7.

Fingers twitching, Nick sent the message. Within seconds, shuffling sounds—footfalls—drew near. He looked down at his phone. Still no confirmation of his text. Did it go through? He strained not to move as the footsteps drew closer. He checked his phone again.

MSG RECVD—DISPOSE OF PHONE.

"KNOCK, KNOCK, KNOCK."

Nick jumped.

"I need you to open the door slowly and come out with your hands raised!" a male voice commanded from outside. "And do it now!"

"Yes, sir." His hand shaking, Nick reached for the door latch. "I'm coming out." He eased open the door. A man in a dark blue suit, white dress shirt, and a burgundy tie pointed a gun at him as he stepped out. The door closed behind him.

"Face on the ground with your arms and legs spread apart!"

As Nick went down to the ground, another man grabbed him and proceeded to do a body search, followed by a scan with a metal detector wand.

"He's clean."

As Nick stood up, the first Secret Service agent thrust his gun back into its holster inside his suit jacket and glared at him, looking him up and down.

"You're one of the people who's supposed to be walking the fairways, spotting balls, right?"

"Yes, sir." Nick dusted himself off, trying to regain his composure. "I just needed to make a quick stop and use the bathroom." His voice trembled. "Not many places to go out here."

"All right, kid." The agent lifted a small walkie-talkie to the side of his face. "All clear." He glanced toward the porta-potty. "We saw someone go in there but didn't have a positive ID." He then looked behind him. "You'd better hustle yourself out there. They're hitting off the tee as we speak."

Suddenly, a distant voice cried out, "FORE!" All three ducked their heads, followed by the clanging of vinyl siding as a stray golf ball caromed off the roof of one of the sheds in the maintenance yard. The ball bounced and rolled to the ground, landing a couple feet from where they stood.

"Nothing like being in the right place at the right time," said the other agent. "Stay out of trouble, kid, and don't go wandering off again." Both agents turned and headed back toward the fairway.

"Yes, sir." Nick gave a long sigh. He glanced back at the bathroom, confident that no one would find the phone where he disposed of it. No one would want to look there.

"Did you see where that shot went?" A caddy, struggling with a golf bag hoisted around his shoulder and noticeably out of breath, came hustling over. Nick immediately recognized him as the president's caddy.

"Right over here." Nick walked toward where the ball had landed.

The caddy strained as he bent down and examined the ball. "Yeah, that's his. Thanks for finding it. I'll take it from here." With a grunt, he unloaded the golf bag and laid it on the ground.

"No problem at all." Nick turned and made his way toward the sixth-hole green. He glanced back and saw the president and his entourage moving toward where he had just come from.

His brush with the Secret Service agents had only temporarily distracted him from the mystery still surrounding the seventh hole. He peered out to his left and could see the flagstick standing over the seventh hole green waiting for them, looking as majestic as always, the spray of ocean water splashing up from the rocks beneath it. Nothing appeared to be out of the ordinary. Everything looked to be as it should. Why then did these people need to know about the president and that hole? Nick was running out of time.

As the last member of the president's foursome finished their putts on the sixth hole, Nick descended the hill and positioned himself along the left side of the seventh hole green. Making the short walk to the seventh tee, the president stopped, reached into his golf bag, and grabbed a club. He would be the first to hit. He bent down to pick up some grass and tossed it in the air to see which way the wind blew. Usually notorious for the strong ocean breezes that can hamper most shots on this hole, the wind remained surprisingly calm. The president peered out over the short par 3, surveying the ground in front of him. He took a couple of practice swings before settling near the ball and taking his stance over it. Aside from the sound of the ocean, all was quiet as the president prepared to take aim at the seventh hole.

CHAPTER 12

"Get us closer, Sergei." Chernov signaled to the other man, motioning for them to move forward.

His phone vibrated in his breast pocket. "Target moving into position," a text message read. He raised a set of binoculars and peered through the lenses, surveying the entire expanse of ocean that surrounded them. He counted three other boats, small sailing crafts, but all a good distance from them. Further out, a group of whales frolicked along the surface, some spraying mists of water from their blowholes. Just beyond there, a Coast Guard ship looked to be heading further out to sea.

Chernov turned to his right and spotted a helicopter circling just offshore, moving away toward the north. As he lowered his binoculars, a wry smile crept to his face. "Fortune seems to be favoring us today, my friend."

Sergei Pacenko and Adrik Chernov had gotten to know each other while serving together in the Russian army. Many years later, when Chernov began his current line of work, he needed someone he could rely on as a partner. Without much in the way of other career prospects and nothing else that could match the kind of money he could make, Pacenko accepted the offer. Since that time, they had formed a successful partnership where each relied on the other's skillset in doing their work.

This operation was no exception. The two men had made all the necessary preparations. They were aware that in situations like this, security protocol usually required a perimeter of about two miles distance from the person or persons being protected. The establishment of such a distance relied on information known about the longest recorded successful rifle shots of highly trained snipers over the last few years. Reports of successful shots ranging from 1-1/4 to 1-1/2 miles over the last several years had been reported from wars in Afghanistan and Iraq. However, some had suggested a Canadian rifleman might have broken all previous records while fighting ISIS in Iraq with a successful shot as long as two miles, though details remained unclear.

Chernov placed little importance on that kind of information. The intelligence on successful Russian sniper shots didn't always get out to the rest of the world. He and others like him had also succeeded at such distances, although they had not received the same kind of international attention. Not such a bad thing, considering the kind of work he did. The more he operated in relative obscurity, the better he could do his job.

Chernov had let his partner know this would be his last assignment. Knowing Pacenko would also be receiving a sizable return for his work, he figured his friend would consider retiring himself or finding another line of work. It was something they would have an opportunity to discuss later. For now, they had a job to do.

Sergei eased up on the throttle of the boat. They had crept to less than two miles from the target and were still closing. Chernov raised his binoculars again and focused them toward the shore. Through the lenses, ocean waves splashed against the rocks beneath the cliff that rose to meet the green grass and white sand traps surrounding the seventh hole.

Chernov shifted toward the middle of the boat and opened a small compartment behind the helm. He made a quick inspection of the gyroscopic stabilizer unit stored there. Though the water was relatively calm that day, the importance of keeping the boat steady could not be overemphasized.

He reached down and lifted the long black bag he had stowed on the floor adjacent to the compartment. Up to this point, he and Pacenko had given the appearance of merely being on a scuba diving trip, complete with dive equipment, wet suits, and other gear. The time had come to set up for what they had really come to do.

He climbed back onto the deck and surveyed across the water with his binoculars. "Stop here."

Pacenko turned off the engine and carefully lowered the anchor into the water.

Chernov unzipped the bag and began extracting the various parts of a long-range sniper rifle. The boat had been modified with a small area on the deck where he could stretch out facedown to better visualize and aim at the target. It also provided sufficient paneling along the sides of the deck so he could not be easily seen.

After positioning the rifle on a bipod mount, he lay out on the deck, rested the right side of his face along the barrel behind the scope, and squinted through the lens. He could see players standing and watching at the seventh hole tee box as one of them prepared to hit a shot.

Pacenko climbed across the deck and squatted behind Chernov. Utilizing both a spotter scope and a wind meter device, he provided wind direction and range data to Chernov, which he, in turn, used to calibrate the rifle.

Chernov peered through the rifle scope again. Not unlike a golfer aiming for the green, he angled his scope toward the flagstick resting directly above the seventh hole. Though this particular method lacked the sophistication of Pacenko's instruments, Chernov could get a pretty good read on the strength and direction of the wind at the target location by merely observing the flag, which, for the moment, remained surprisingly still.

"Very little wind today, Sergei." Chernov chuckled as he looked back over his shoulder at Pacenko. "Like I said, fortune continues to smile on us—at least for now." He returned his eye to the scope. "But she can be a fickle thing."

Pacenko checked his instruments. "Yes, and so can the wind." He jerked his head up and looked out across the water and toward the shore. "I suggest we do this thing before they both change on us."

Chernov gripped the rifle and slipped his index finger into the space between the trigger guard and the trigger. Early evening approached, the sun dipping below some clouds hugging the western horizon along the Pacific Ocean. Chernov still had plenty of daylight to spot his target. Through the scope, he watched the first player of the group reach back with his club and strike at the ball, his arms then carrying across his body on his follow-through. The player handed the club back to his caddie and positioned himself to the side as the other players prepared their shots. He appeared to be about six feet tall, wearing a maroon-colored pullover, gray pants, and a San Francisco Giants baseball cap, just as an earlier text had described. Chernov narrowed his eyes and focused intently through the lens to get a better view of the player's face.

"Target identified," Chernov announced. He moved the rifle slightly until the crosshairs of the gunsight rested squarely on the person of the president of the United States.

Having instructed both Joe and Luke to remain in the cabin while he and other park personnel searched for Pete, Leo hurried toward the cove. He found the small outboard motorboat owned by the park authority tied up in the cove. As he loosened the line that connected the boat to the wooden piling, his hands seemed to operate separately from the rest of his body. He could hardly believe everything had come to this. But he also realized he could no longer keep his head in the sand and pretend that this didn't directly involve him. Perhaps he should have done something a long time ago, but he could make up for it now. He had to get to Chernov's boat as quickly as possible. What he would do when he got there, he didn't know. He'd have to figure it out along the way.

The engine roared to life with one yank on the pull cord, and he veered the boat toward the ocean. As he exited the mouth of the cove, he glanced to the shoreline for any sign of Pete. Seeing nothing other than the panorama of brush, trees, and crashing waves against the rocks, he could only hope the other park personnel would find him. For now, the only thought on his mind was stopping Adrik Chernov.

Nick stood in the tall grass of the rough, several yards from the seventh hole green. He continued searching for whatever might alert him to why the people he was working for wanted to know when the president would be at that hole. So far, nothing had jumped out at him. But there had to be something.

He thought about what his role had been in helping these people. It had been nothing like he expected. Told by Yuri that he would be gathering all sorts of information about the president's golf game—how he plays, who he plays with, whether he bends the rules in his favor. But nothing like that had been asked of him. It seemed the only thing they wanted to know had to do with identifying the president and alerting them to his approach on the seventh hole. Almost as if they were merely asking him to help lead the president toward some purpose here. But what?

He looked up at the tee area where one of the players hit a shot that landed between two of the sand bunkers. The hole, with a small green surrounded on all sides by the ocean, left little room for error. Once on the green, it was probably the most isolated and exposed area on the golf course.

The most isolated and exposed—Nick glanced to the left, to the right, and scanned everything in between. A knot began tightening in his stomach. The president now entered a place without the slightest cover or protection, an area that jutted out into a vast openness in every direction.

The people Nick worked for weren't interested in information about the president. They simply wanted Nick to lead the president right to this very spot. And that's exactly what he had done.

Nick was suddenly struck by the worst possible thought. Could these people be attempting to bring harm to the president? Had the people he'd been feeding information to been devising a plan from the beginning? Was someone watching and waiting for just the right moment to act? Had he helped lead the president into a trap?

Nick glanced up toward the tee area again. The players began the few steps down to the green. The president led the way, strolling toward one of the sand bunkers where his ball had landed.

Nick thought about his brother Yuri. He couldn't imagine him being part of a sinister plot, much less getting his kid brother involved. Maybe the people Yuri worked for also wanted to use him, purposely keeping him in the dark about the real purpose of the assignment.

Nick remembered happier days at Holy Transfiguration Russian Orthodox Church, where he and Yuri attended Sunday Divine Liturgy together with their family and where they went to the same parish school. Though three years apart, they often served on the altar together during church services.

Those formative years had given him a sense of the sacred ... the idea of a higher power. He had learned the Ten Commandments and knew the difference between right and wrong. He also knew that one of those commandments required him to uphold and protect the dignity of every human life.

He wanted to do something. But what? Images flashed in his mind of the dream he had of the president on a golf course, staring at him, his hands reaching out, a look of distress on his face. Secret Service agents all around, wrestling Nick to the ground and rushing to the president. And now, the scene before him became eerily similar.

More than a premonition, a hunch, or even intuition, Nick was now thoroughly convinced this was not a dream—the president was in danger. He peered out toward the ocean. A helicopter flew a good distance to his right—no doubt keeping far enough away to avoid bothering the players. Although nothing seemed out of the ordinary, an overwhelming sense of dread gripped him as he viewed the vast open space the president now walked into.

What a cool place! Pete found himself along the water's edge of China Cove. He had made his way down from a place further up the trail they hadn't explored earlier. Seeing it up close made it even more spectacular than just seeing it from the cliffs above. He stood on a narrow pocket of sandy white beach surrounded by walls of rock formations where the ocean formed a tidal pool of emerald green, crystal-clear water. He had read about enchanting places like this where one might expect to see a mermaid sitting on one of the rocks. He could see a small sea cave and rock arch just beyond the beach to his left. With the low tide, the cave appeared to be accessible by foot, just above the water's edge.

As he looked around, he suddenly caught sight of something moving. A more studied glance revealed a young boy peering out at him from the cave. Pete moved to his right for a better view. As he did, the boy backed away from the mouth of the cave. Pete stopped and continued looking. Suddenly, the boy appeared again. With a headband made of simple cloth tied around long jet-black hair and dressed only in an animal skin loincloth, he appeared to be Native American. A necklace of small seashells dangled from around his neck and rested on his chest.

The boy raised his hand and waved it back and forth as if indicating for Pete to come to the cave. Pete looked behind him, thinking the boy may have been signaling someone else. Not seeing anyone, Pete looked back, but the boy had disappeared. Hesitating for a moment, he thought about Joe and his brother, Luke, who had to be wondering about him.

He looked toward the cave again. A few more minutes of exploring couldn't hurt anyone. Pete moved along the rock wall of the cove to his left and out toward the cave. As he drew nearer, Pete thought he heard voices from inside the cave, but he couldn't be sure.

Light flickered on the inside walls of the entrance to the cave. He peered in but could only make out shadows of movements. As he entered, the boy suddenly appeared in front of him. He took Pete by the hand and led him further inside. As he focused ahead, he noticed the light came from a couple of small torches placed along parts of the interior walls. As his eyes grew more accustomed to the surroundings, he was startled to discover ten or twelve men gathered in front of him in what appeared to be the furthest extent of the cave.

One by one, they turned their attention toward him. He stood there feeling a bit uneasy, but then each of them offered him a sign of greeting. They smiled and extended their hands as if to welcome him. Like the boy, they all appeared to be Native American. Though they spoke in a language he didn't understand, he was made to feel like one of them. Pete noticed each of the men holding a crude, primitive cutting tool. Scrapes and holes marred the walls as if they'd been extracting something.

The boy led Pete to a lumpy mound covered in animal skins and shrouded in darkness. He shifted to allow the torchlight to fall on it. Wanting to know what lay hidden, he stooped and reached for the skins, but then he hesitated and glanced at the boy for permission. The boy gestured for him to continue, so he peeled the skins back. And he gasped. Large nuggets with a dusting of black sand from the cave walls formed a sizable pile. Flecks glittered in the torchlight, flecks of what looked like ... pure gold!

One of the men approached Pete and handed him something heavy in a small wrapping. Pete opened it and found another large quantity of gold. "Wow!" He'd never held a chunk of gold before.

The man pointed to the gold and then to Pete as if he wanted Pete to have it. With a smile, the man waved his hand toward the cave walls all around them, showing Pete the plentiful supply of the precious material that existed there—as if to say it could be shared by all.

Pete's eyes widened with astonishment. Perhaps it was true after all, what he had read about the legend of the Ohlone Indians who once lived here. The story suggested that when Father Serra established Mission San Carlos Borromeo in nearby Carmel, men of the Ohlone tribe, themselves members of the mission, found large amounts of gold in the black sand within the walls of the caves under Point Lobos.

Pete stood mystified, hardly able to believe what he saw. Could this be another deposit of that same gold? How much gold was in here? All this gold—his attention shifted back to the man who stood before him and then to the others. Such good and generous people, they seemed happy to share what they'd found. What would happen to them should others discover this place? Would they be taken advantage of? No—he would not let that happen!

The boy grabbed Pete's arm and tugged him back toward the cave entrance. Before he had a chance to say goodbye and thank the men for their extraordinary kindness, Pete found himself outside the cave. He turned around, but the boy had vanished. A bit confused, he stretched his neck and peered into the cave again but saw no light and heard no voices.

He gazed out toward the ocean as thin rays of fading light from the late setting sun angled through spaces between the large surrounding rocks. Suddenly, he remembered Luke and Joe and how they would probably be looking for him. Pulling out his phone from his pocket, he noticed the battery had died. Not wasting another minute, he began the climb back up the slope along the slippery rocks and to the trail above. But wait. He had left the gold behind. He had to go back. He quickly turned and ...

Leo spotted Chernov's boat a couple hundred yards ahead of him. He shifted the outboard motor handle and angled the boat in that direction, pushing hard on the throttle. Could he get there in time?

Suddenly, a call came through on his radio. A member of the search team informed him that Pete had been found on the rocks between Gibson Beach and China Cove. It appeared as if he slipped and hit his head. He had been unconscious for a short time but seemed to be okay. Paramedics were on their way and planned to take him to Community Hospital in Monterey.

"Good news," Leo responded. "Make sure to notify Luke's brother and friend at the Whalers Cabin." He hesitated for a moment. "I'm in the rescue boat but should be back shortly. Over and out." He set the radio down and returned his focus to the matter at hand.

His heart pounded rapidly in his chest as the distance between him and Chernov's boat continued to close. As he approached, he saw something strange. One of the men lay prone on the deck, looking away from him. The other man crouched behind him, holding something in his hands. With little or no time left, he knew what he had to do. Pushing on the throttle, Leo aimed straight for the other boat.

The president found his ball sitting in the sand trap in front of the green. He laughed as he traded quips with the other players. None of them seemed the least bit concerned about the imminent danger, which Nick no longer doubted. He noticed a couple of Secret Service agents spread out along the back end of the green that faced the ocean, but they hardly seemed like much of a barrier between the president and anyone intent upon doing him harm.

The president hit a sand wedge from the trap and watched the ball trickle past the hole, finally resting on the edge of the other side of the green.

Nick cringed. This would expose the president even more, bringing him about as close to the oceanfront as he could be.

The president strolled across the green, bent down, and placed a marker behind his ball. He stepped back and removed his hat. Turning, he gazed out over the ocean. "Fellas, have you ever seen a prettier sight?"

Chernov's eye focused through the scope of his rifle. The president of the United States stood squarely in his crosshairs. "Bull's eye!" he whispered. He began to gently press the forefinger of his right hand against the trigger. Chernov lay completely still as he slowly took in a breath and prepared to fire.

CHAPTER 13

Nick inched closer to the green. His heart pounded, and his stomach clenched. Unwilling to wait another second and hoping an idea would come to his head, he sprung forward, striding toward the president.

As if watching a scene from a movie, everything seemed to move in slow motion. Out of the corner of his eye, he glimpsed Secret Service agents advancing toward him. It was the only thing he could do. He opened his mouth and shouted, “GET DOWN, MR. PRESIDENT!”

The roar of an approaching motorboat jarred Pacenko’s attention. With a rush of wind whipping his hair across his face, he spun around to see the park ranger in a boat speeding right toward him—about to ram into them! He turned back to warn Chernov, who hadn’t moved from his prone position on the deck.

Two sounds broke the relative calm of the early evening of the Monterey Peninsula. The crack of a gunshot. The crash of boats colliding. Pacenko sailed forward at the impact, breathless as he plunged into the numbing cool water of the ocean. Panic-stricken, he fought his way to the surface and gulped in air. Water blurring his vision, he saw Chernov no longer on the deck but clinging to the railing of the boat.

Nick raced across the green. Something sliced through the air, whizzing past his head—too close—striking something nearby with a *thunk*. Just as he reached the president, a Secret Service agent tackled Nick to the ground. Other agents surrounded the president, who lay motionless under them. More people rushed over, creating a shield around the president.

Leo found himself tossed forward in his boat but managed to recover himself. Though the front of the boat was twisted and bent, it remained afloat, and he could still work the motor. He peered into the other boat just as Chernov got up and came toward him with a pistol in his hand. Leo quickly turned the boat hard and pressed the throttle.

Chernov took aim as shots rang out.

Ducking, Leo sped away.

"Thank God, Pete's okay," Joe said as they headed to Luke's car in the Whalers Cove parking lot.

"You're not kidding. He really had me worried for a while." Luke felt for the keys in his pocket. "I know the hospital in Monterey where they're taking him. We'll meet him there."

As they neared the car, the cove came into view. A boat sped toward the entrance to the cove in front of them.

"Who do you think that is?" Luke said, pointing.

Joe looked up. "I don't know."

Although darkness had begun settling in around the cove, it didn't hide the damage to the front end of the boat. The person inside slumped over, not appearing to be in control of the vessel. As they watched, the boat slammed into small rocks along the shoreline and came to a jarring stop.

Luke and Joe sprinted toward the beach, Luke reaching the boat first. A man lay on the floor of the boat. Blood partially covered the name "Leo Verenich" on the nametag. Luke bent down closer.

Joe came running up behind Luke. "Is he hurt?"

"I'm afraid so." Luke placed his fingers along the man's neck in hopes of getting a pulse. "It's the park ranger from the cabin. He's alive but in pretty bad shape. It looks like he's been shot."

Leo slowly opened his eyes. "I-I've got to get to the cabin." He grabbed ahold of the side of the boat, swaying as he tried pulling himself up.

Luke took hold of his arm and steadied him. "We've got to get you to a hospital."

Another boat approached the cove, the steady roar of its motor growing louder. A spotlight from the boat danced along the rocks, searching along the beachfront.

"We've got to get out of here," Leo demanded in a pained voice. The spotlight suddenly trained on them, gunshots rang out, and bullets ricocheted off the rocks all around them.

"Get me to my feet."

Luke and Joe lifted Leo and helped carry him to Luke's car.

A bullet caromed off the top of the car as Luke started the engine. "Stay down!" He turned the wheel and pressed his foot hard on the accelerator as they whirled out of the parking lot.

"Stop by the cabin! Stop by the cabin!" Leo called out. "These are bad men, and they are after something hidden there." He grabbed Luke's arm from the back seat. "You've got to do this!"

Luke hit the brakes, and the car came to an abrupt stop behind the cabin. He turned toward Leo. "Where is this thing?"

Leo coughed, trying to regain his voice.

"Tell us quickly before we all get killed!"

"The old gray cypress tree ... just to the side of the front door ..." Leo gasped for air, his voice becoming weaker. "You'll find a big black bag. Hidden."

Luke turned toward Joe. "Keep an eye on him—I'll be right back."

Luke swung open the driver's door and bolted to the front of the cabin. Just inside the door stood a tree—old and twisted, like many of the cypress trees in this part of California. He reached inside an opening in the trunk of the tree and lifted out a large black bag, just as Leo had described. Although heavier than he had expected, he managed to throw it over his shoulder and start toward the car.

He hurled the bag across the driver's seat, where Joe grabbed it and shoved it in the backseat next to Leo. Back in his seat, Luke glanced in the rearview mirror. Headlights moved swiftly toward them.

Luke shifted the car into drive and sped out of the parking lot as fast as he could. He charged toward the park's exit, the other vehicle not far behind. The sound of gunfire echoed through the trees on both sides of the road, flashes of light behind them. A bullet struck the rear of the car, shattering a taillight. Luke sped to where the road intersected with the Pacific Coast Highway. The traffic moved from his right to left ahead of him, but nothing came from his left. He turned hard to his right, the car screeching across the pavement and glancing off a car that had come to a stop in the opposite lane. Without slowing down, Luke regained control of the vehicle, getting back in the lane. Cars honked in protest. Luke glanced in the rearview mirror. A pickup truck also made the turn, speeding along behind them.

"What is going on?" Luke glared at Leo through the rearview mirror as he raced down the highway. "Who are these guys, and why is this bag so important?"

Hunched over in his seat, Leo clutched his shoulder and winced. Slowly, he lifted his head. "They're assassins, sent to take out the president," he said in a low voice.

"*What?*" Joe asked.

"It's true. And ... God help us ... they may have succeeded." Leo stopped and coughed, his face contorting. After a moment, he struggled to catch his breath and then continued. "There's a great deal of money in this bag. It's their payout. If they get it, they may not ever get caught."

Luke glanced in the mirror, the pickup truck gaining on them. Suddenly, a car in front slowed down. Luke turned sharply. Losing control, the car veered just off the road, scraping the guardrail, the only thing between them and a precipitous drop to the Pacific Ocean below. Luke quickly turned back onto the road, his heart in his throat.

Joe straightened in his seat. "Boy, that was close!"

"We're in the Big Sur," Leo uttered in a low voice. "It can be treacherous through here."

Luke glanced at Leo through the rearview mirror. "You're not kidding." The mirror showed him more than just Leo. The headlights of the truck chasing them darted back and forth on the two-lane road, moving closer.

Another bullet glanced off the back of the car, causing both Joe and Leo to drop down in their seats. Luke scooted as low as he could while still being able to drive. Just ahead, a sign read *Bixby Canyon Bridge—Drive with Caution.*

He'd driven along this stretch of the Pacific Coast Highway before. Bixby Bridge was an iconic tourist destination where people liked to pull off the side of the road and take in the view, especially during sunsets. The bridge featured a distinctive arch design and rose above a canyon that opened out into the Pacific Ocean. As darkness descended upon the coastline, people returned to their cars along the side of the highway near the bridge.

Traffic in front of them made it difficult to pass anyone. Luke had no other choice but to slow down. Pull-off areas existed on both sides of the highway as they approached the bridge. The area to the right had very little room between the roadside surface and the side of the cliff. As they began to cross the span, Luke looked again in the mirror. The pickup truck had caught up to them. Its headlights illuminated the interior of Luke's car as it sped forward. Joe shielded his eyes as he glanced behind him. "He's not slowing down!"

"Hold on!" Luke shouted as he braced for impact. He glanced in the mirror. Another car suddenly pulled out behind them from the side of the road. It moved directly in the path of the speeding pickup truck. The sound of screeching tires, breaking glass, and crashing metal caused everyone to quickly look behind them. Luke continued moving slowly forward, following the cars in front of him. Another glance in the mirror made his breath catch. The car behind them spun around before coming to a stop. Its front bumper and fenders twisted. Smoke rose up from beneath a crumpled hood.

From the corner of his eye, he saw headlights moving erratically to his right and behind him, They disappeared suddenly, dipping into the darkness of the ravine below the bridge.

Gripping the steering wheel and trying to stay focused, Luke glanced at Joe, who was looking out in the same direction through the passenger side window. "Did you see that?"

Joe's mouth gaped open—his eyes wide. "I-I-I'm not real sure." His voice trembled. "But I think somebody just went off the road and over the bridge."

"Was it a car or a truck?"

"I couldn't tell."

Leo coughed as he struggled to speak. "Keep moving," he said, his voice becoming more guttural. "We can't know for sure. They could still be after us."

Luke gazed through the mirror again. A couple of vehicles started moving behind them.

Leo coughed and slouched in his seat.

"We need to get him to a hospital," Joe said.

"*Out here?*" Luke bellowed, his voice raised. "The closest hospital is in the opposite direction ... and we can't do that. Not to mention we're heading into one of the most remote areas of the state."

Luke's car picked up speed again. A line of headlights moved steadily behind them.

"Unfortunately, I think Leo is right," Luke said. He and Joe exchanged glances. "We've got to keep moving until we know for sure they're not following."

Joe turned around in his seat. "Leo?" Joe leaned toward the backseat. "Hey, can you hear me?"

Luke glanced, but the darkness hid Leo. "How is he?"

"He's still breathing, but I think he's passed out. There's a lot of blood around his shoulder area."

"Try your phone again. Maybe we can get a hold of somebody who can help us."

"I've been trying. I haven't had a good signal out here since earlier today, and almost nothing since we got on the highway."

Luke kept looking in the mirror for any sign of the pickup truck. "Either they're still after us, or they went over the bridge. Either way, we need to get some help."

Joe put his phone down, shaking his head.

"Still nothing, huh?" Luke asked.

"No. But I've been thinking about Mission San Antonio. We're heading in that general direction, aren't we?"

"Yeah, but the mission is further down and on the other side of these mountains." Luke pointed to his left through the driver's side window. "These cliffs are part of the St. Lucia Mountain range that separates the coastline from the interior regions where the mission is." He shook his head. "Besides, I haven't seen a single intersecting road that could get us over there, anyway." He peered down the road. With few streetlights along the winding curves of the highway, the darkness made it difficult to see too far ahead. "And even if we somehow got there, who's going to be able to help us?"

"The friars, of course," Joe answered without hesitation.

"You think they'll still be there?"

"Only one way to find out. Sounds like we don't have too many other options."

Luke shook his head. "The only problem is how to get there."

Joe held up his phone. "I downloaded an off-line map earlier today. Whenever I go hiking somewhere, I like to download a map of the area we're going to, just in case I need it."

"You sure chose the right day for that. Good job." Luke reached over and patted Joe on the shoulder. "Let's see how good it works."

Joe studied his phone. "There's a road a few miles down that looks like it can take us through the mountains. It's called Nacimiento-Fergusson Road."

"Sounds familiar." Luke thought back to the last time he came down this way with some of his Marine buddies a few months ago. "If it's the same one I remember, it's one of the only roads down this way that connects with the highway."

Joe turned on the car radio. "Maybe I can find a station that can tell us something about what might have happened to the president."

Luke could only focus on the road. "Tough getting a station out here, though."

After working the radio dial, Joe was picking up little more than dead air and soft static, but he kept trying. "Hard to believe only last year Pete and I went to Camp David and met with the president."

Luke nodded. "I remember." Even though he couldn't be there, Luke recalled the momentous events that occurred at his alma mater, Westthorpe Academy, and how they had caught the president's attention. He could only imagine the effect the speculation about the president was having on Joe.

"I know you and the president share a lot in common about the faith."

Joe nodded his head. "Yeah, he takes his faith very seriously. He has a strong devotion to the Blessed Mother."

"That's a comforting thought." Luke eased off the gas as a road sign came into view. Nope. Not the right road yet. He glanced in the rearview mirror, worried that the men who had been chasing them could still be back there, trying to catch up. He wouldn't be able to relax until he knew for sure.

The scratchy but audible voice of a woman could just be heard through the car speakers. "That sounds like something." Luke pointed toward the radio. "Go back a little." Joe adjusted the knob. "There it is."

> Sources from Pebble Beach Golf Course report that an incident has occurred there involving the president of the United States. Unfortunately, no other details are known at this time. The president arrived there late this afternoon for a scheduled round of golf after concluding his trip to the G7 Summit in San Francisco. As soon as further details are made available, we will let you know.

Luke turned his head toward Joe. "It looks like Leo was right."

Joe sat back. "The president really needs our prayers."

They prayed an *Our Father*, a *Hail Mary*, and a *Glory Be* for the president, for Leo, for his brother Pete, and for themselves. Joe offered an additional prayer, asking for the help of Our Lady of Lourdes.

A sign indicated Nacimiento-Fergusson Road just ahead. "That's the one we want." Luke eased on the brakes and peeked in the mirror again. Although he hadn't noticed anything unusual behind him for the last couple of miles, he still needed to be cautious. He purposely didn't use the turn signal, and he made a quick left onto Nacimiento-Fergusson Road.

"Here we go." After completing a sharp turn, Luke centered the car in the lane. "The Coast Highway is dicey enough, but this road may be even worse." Stretching his neck forward, he peered up through the windshield. "We've got some climbs to get through and a narrow, winding road ahead, so keep the prayers going."

Suddenly, the car hit a deep pothole, jolting everyone in their seats. Joe turned behind him and reached back toward Leo. "He seems to barely be breathing." He returned to his seat. "If we don't get help soon, I think we're going to lose him."

"I hear you, Joe." Headlights reflected in the rearview mirror. "Another vehicle just turned onto the road with us."

They soon entered a stretch of road that meandered through a heavily wooded area. A flickering light that would suddenly disappear and then appear again zigzagged through the trees behind them.

"Do you think it's them?" Joe asked, his voice taut.

Luke gripped the steering wheel with both hands. "I don't know." He focused squarely on the road ahead of them. "I only know that there isn't anything on this road between here and where we're going." He paused. "If it is, it's just them and us out here."

CHAPTER 14

The road curved through the mountains with sharp turns and steep climbs. The headlights of Luke's car only partially penetrated the darkness in front of them, the view made worse by patches of fog that began descending on the mountain. Some areas of the road offered only enough room for a single car to get through. The lack of guardrails made it even more dangerous with nothing to stop a car from going over the side of a cliff should it get too close to the edge.

Luke was at least relieved to know that, for the last couple of miles, there had been no sign of the vehicle that had been following them. After continuing up the side of the mountain, the road leveled off a bit. They had reached the top of the climb and found themselves on the mountain above the fog and some low-lying clouds. An opening in the woods offered a spectacular view of a starry nighttime sky over a valley and the Pacific Ocean. The moon hung close to the horizon and reflected on the distant waters. As Luke took in the breathtaking sight, he could forget, at least for a moment, the reason that had brought them to this place and the desperate situation they found themselves in.

"Oh, no!" Luke glanced over the edge of the road and down into the valley below them. After not seeing anything for a while, he could not ignore what appeared to be headlights through the mist, winding their way along the road and up the mountain.

"What is it?" Joe asked.

"Looks like we've got company, again. Not far behind us." Luke gripped the steering wheel with both hands and eased his foot down more firmly on the accelerator. Gradually, the car picked up speed. "We'll be making our way down the other side of the mountain and can hopefully gain some ground on them."

The road flattened out for the next couple of miles as the car surged through another heavily wooded section. Luke kept glancing in the mirror, watching for the other vehicle. He rubbed his eyes. Fatigue, stress, and not having stopped after many miles of driving wore on him.

"You all right, Luke?"

"I'm better now that we're out of the mountains. Those were some nasty turns."

A small glimmer of light flashed in Luke's mirror, then disappeared. He swerved the car a bit as he worked another bend in the road. "Thought I saw something back there."

Joe turned and looked behind them. "I see it!"

Luke looked behind them again. A distant light blinked in and out through the trees, only to vanish again. "Keep looking, Joe."

As they picked up speed, the terrain gave way to fewer trees and a wider range of visibility.

"How far to the mission from here?" Luke asked.

Joe studied his phone. "A little more than seven miles." He paused. "In about four and a half miles, we want to make a slight left turn onto Del Venturi Road."

The moon had risen over the mountains, becoming more visible now that they had left the woods behind them. It almost seemed to be following them, providing an eerie glow through what remained of the nighttime mist. The pale light revealed a shadowy landscape of rolling hills and open meadows dotted with ghost-like figures of gnarled trees covered in Spanish moss.

Out of the woods and on a straighter road, Luke figured it wouldn't take long to know for sure if someone was following them. Within seconds, a set of headlights appeared in his mirror, bounding over the hill and out of the woods, speeding toward them. "There he is."

Joe turned and looked. "Yeah, and he's coming fast."

Luke struggled to keep the car on the road as it picked up speed. "How close are we to the turn?"

Joe checked his phone. "A little more than a mile." He looked behind him again. "They're closing on us."

Luke strained his eyes further ahead on the road. "I'm gonna have trouble seeing the turn. Let me know when we're near it."

"It looks like there'll be a split in the road where you'll bear left. Point four miles." Joe glanced up. They sped toward a clump of trees where the road split off. "This is it!"

Luke jerked the steering wheel to the left. The car slid off the road and straight toward some trees. He slammed on the brakes, and the car jerked to a stop perpendicular to the road. They both looked up. The headlights of the other vehicle bore down on them.

Luke stomped on the accelerator. The car's tires screeched back onto the road surface, and they headed up Del Venturi Road. Luke watched through the mirror to see what direction the vehicle behind them would go. It didn't take long before the headlights turned onto the same road behind them.

"These guys are relentless." He looked at Joe. "I just remembered we're coming up close to Fort Hunter Liggett."

"The Army base?"

"Yeah. Hopefully, somebody there might also be able to help us."

Joe looked down at his phone again. "In about two and a half miles, you wanna make a left onto Mission Road."

For the first time in a while, Luke could now see a haze of light in front of them, not too far in the distance ... indications of civilization. After miles of nothing but darkness, it seemed like a mirage.

"That's got to be Fort Hunter Liggett," Luke blurted. "The problem is, they don't take kindly to strange cars speeding through their perimeter. Not to mention, they do a lot of live-ammo training out here. I'd just as soon avoid having a howitzer shell fired into the front grill of the car."

As they drew closer, the light came into greater focus. A couple of streetlights illumined the intersection in front of them.

"Left up here," Joe called out.

Luke turned sharply into the opposite turn lane of the intersection, kicking up dust from the side of the road. The other vehicle fell directly behind them as they sped down Mission Road.

Darkness enveloped them again. No streetlights extended to that portion of the road. Luke strained to make out shapes in the blackness. The turn to the mission had to be there.

"There it is!" Joe pointed across the windshield.

With a slight turn of the wheel, Luke drove onto the entrance road of the mission grounds. Their pursuers followed, almost touching Luke's rear bumper. Suddenly, headlights revealed several deer scampering directly in front of them.

"Look out!" Joe shouted.

Luke slammed on the brakes and turned sharply. The car slid off the road and across the dirt, crashing head-on into an old stone well that stood near the front of the mission.

Garbled voices surrounded Joe as if in a dream. Hands took hold of his arms and legs and lifted him up. He opened his eyes a little but could not distinguish anything through the darkness. His neck ached as the strangers carried him a short distance to a room illuminated by a very dim light.

Lowered gently onto a rather hard and narrow bed with a thin pillow under his head, he opened his mouth in an attempt to speak. Nothing came out. With some effort, he eased his head toward the light but could only see shadows moving about. Shifting his gaze to the floor, he noticed simple leather sandals on the feet of the people in the room. Voices spoke softly in a foreign language ... Spanish?

He tried moving his arms and legs but found them too stiff and sore. As he struggled to sit himself up, a hand touched his shoulder.

"Now, now, my son," said a familiar voice. "You must rest after what you've been through."

Joe opened and closed his eyes, straining to see more clearly. He began to make out the image of someone next to him, alongside the bed. It appeared to be a man in a gray religious habit with a hood covering most of his head. A large *Mallorcan* crucifix hung from his neck and rested on the front of his habit.

"Father," uttered Joe, rather feebly. He gazed at the face of the old padre.

"God be with you, my son." The old padre spoke in a gentle voice as he slowly nodded his head and smiled reassuringly.

Joe took in his surroundings. "Where am I?"

"Why, you are in the Mission San Antonio de Padua, of course."

Joe tried to sit up again, but his head spun with the attempt, and his arms wouldn't cooperate.

"You must rest, my son." Father eased him back onto the bed. "You have been through quite an ordeal that has required great courage and sacrifice."

Joe wanted to speak but again found he didn't have the strength to even open his mouth. For the moment, he could only lie on the bed and listen to the padre.

"You know, when I was about your age, I read a very popular novel of that time called *Las Sergas de Esplandián*, or, as you would say in your English, *The Adventures of Esplandián*." The old padre's eyes sparkled, and his face radiated. "That book introduced me to the name *California*. It described it as a mythical place filled with wonder and enchantment. Esplandián was a very brave and chivalrous knight who fought to defend truth and honor."

An extraordinary peace and otherworldliness overcame Joe as he listened to the padre, something he couldn't quite understand or describe—not unlike what he experienced during their first meeting. He glanced around the room and noticed its simplicity and plainness. A single burning candle on top of a small wooden table provided the only source of light. A single crucifix over the bed and a simple gray habit hung on the otherwise bare walls. The padre sat in the only chair in the room.

"When some of my fellow countrymen first came to this part of the world, it reminded them of the California mentioned in the book, so that is what they called it." The padre paused for a moment. "I remember when they first told me that I would be leading my brother friars to California, how joyful we became in thanking Almighty God."

Joe could see in the padre a youthfulness and innocence about him that likely endeared him to everyone he met.

"But my greatest joy, of course, was in knowing that I, unworthy priest that I am, would have the great blessing of bringing the gospel message of God's love to the people here." This brought a broad smile to the padre's face.

He placed his hand on Joe's arm. "In many ways, you and your friends, with what you have done today, remind me of Esplandián and his brave knights."

Father leaned back in his chair. "The world is in great need of such people. The events of today have demonstrated just how vulnerable the world can be to those who wish to bring division and conflict."

At Father's mention of his friends, Joe again struggled to speak. He wanted to know what had become of Luke and Leo, but he couldn't utter the words.

Father must have noticed his frustration. "All in God's time," he said. "All you need do is trust in him."

The padre turned toward the window, where a sliver of pale light streamed into the room through the partially opened shutters.

"I see it is already morning, and I have just remembered it is my turn today to ring the mission bells— one of my favorite duties." Father extended his arms out in a sign of welcoming. "Soon, it will be time to gather everyone to the mission for prayer and to prepare for the many tasks we are called to do this day." Father gave Joe a smile. "For the moment, I must leave you. But you are in very capable hands, my young Esplandián." The padre then took Joe's left hand and placed something in it. "There is no more powerful a means at our disposal than the gift of prayer." He closed Joe's hand and covered it gently with one of his own. "And how can our Blessed Lord say no to His Holy Mother when we ask her for her help through the praying of the Rosary?"

Joe opened his hand, discovering a beautiful set of handcrafted wooden rosary beads. He ran his fingers over the smooth beads. Between each set of ten beads was a larger bead made of turquoise, all held together by colorful pieces of coral. On the end, dangled a simple but carefully crafted small wooden cross.

"These were a gift made and given to me by one of the Indian families at the Mission San Carlos Borromeo in Carmel." Father looked at the beads admiringly. "I would like you to have them."

Overwhelmed by the padre's generosity, Joe shook his head and tried handing the rosary beads back. He wanted to tell him he couldn't possibly accept such a gift but still found himself too weak to express it.

Father closed Joe's hand again with the rosary beads inside. "I insist that you keep them for the journey ahead. More work is always required of us in cultivating the vineyard of the Lord. As the gospel reminds us, the harvest is plentiful, but the laborers are few."

Joe found it difficult to argue about anything with the padre. Besides, Joe's present condition made it virtually impossible to offer any objection. He rested his hand on the bed and found himself instinctively holding some of the beads of the rosary between his thumb and his index finger.

Father got up. As he lifted himself from the chair, Joe noticed him favoring one leg, something Joe remembered him doing when first seeing him in the mission chapel.

"We will meet again very soon, I promise you." Father raised his hand over Joe to offer his priestly blessing.

"*Per intercessionem beatae Mariae semper Virginis, et Sancte Ioseph; Benedictio Dei Omnipotentis, Patris, et Filii, et Spiritus Sancti, descendat super te et maneat semper. Amen.*"

As Father spoke the words, Joe found himself returning to that place of serenity and peacefulness he had experienced before. He closed his eyes and followed the words, remembering from his Latin studies.

"*Through the intercession of the Blessed Virgin Mary and Saint Joseph; may the blessing of Almighty God, Father, Son, and Holy Spirit descend upon you and remain with you forever. Amen.*"

Joe suddenly heard his own voice in a whispered tone saying, "Thank you, Father Serra."

"God be with you, my son."

He gradually opened his eyes again and looked around the room, finding no one there. More light filtered through the shutters of the window. The candle on the table no longer burned. In fact—Joe did a doubletake—it didn't appear to have ever been lit.

Before he could process that, the mission bells rang. The friars would now be gathering for morning prayer.

Joe tried moving again, but his body resisted. Thoughts of Luke, Pete, Leo, the president all seemed jumbled in his mind. What had happened to them? He decided to do the one thing he knew he could do—pray. He felt for the rosary beads, but as he did, his eyelids grew heavy. He struggled to stay awake, but he could no longer fight it. The mission bells continued to ring, calling the monks to prayer as Joe drifted to sleep.

CHAPTER 15

"Mr. Pryce, can you hear me?" came a feminine voice.

Joe tried opening his eyes, but the bright light hurt, so he closed them again and listened to his surroundings. Who was in the room with him? The voice didn't sound familiar.

"Mr. Pryce," the woman repeated.

"Yes," Joe answered, almost inaudibly, as he struggled to find his voice.

"Do you know where you are, Mr. Pryce?"

Wanting to sit up, Joe tried moving his arms but found one of them connected to ... an intravenous tube? He forced his eyes open this time, blinking as they adjusted to the light.

He lay in a bed in a white room that smelled of antiseptic. Windows lined one wall, overlooking a hallway where a few figures milled about. An IV bag hung from a nearby stand, an overbed table beside it. A dark-haired woman in a navy-blue windbreaker jacket stood alongside the bed to his left. Yellow letters on the top left of the jacket identified her—*FBI*.

Still trying to orient himself to his surroundings, Joe tried turning his head, but a brace around his neck limited his mobility.

The woman stepped back, pressed the touch screen of a cell phone, and raised it to her ear. "He's awake," she announced to someone on the other end. Without acknowledging Joe at all, she turned away and stepped to the door. Then she whispered something to a police officer in the hallway, a big man Joe hadn't seen before. He turned and looked at Joe with a hardened expression as the woman joined him in the hallway and closed the door.

Joe watched through the glass wall that overlooked the corridor. People in suits, police uniforms, and medical garb, some talking and others looking in at him, made Joe wish the windows had a curtain.

How had he gotten here? And what was up with the police guard and the FBI? Hey, maybe he could find something out about Luke and Leo, and ... he hesitated to even think about the president, considering everything that had happened. Perhaps that explained all the security personnel outside. Maybe they discovered the connection between what happened to the president and the men chasing them. But why wouldn't they tell him what was going on? Had his parents been informed of all this? And what about Pete back in the hospital in Monterey?

Joe thought back to all that had happened since the last time he saw Pete at Point Lobos. He suddenly realized he had lost all track of time—or of days—for that matter. Constrained by the neck brace, he shifted his gaze to the window. Light filtered in around the edges of drawn blinds. Then he glanced around the room as best he could but saw no phone or television. An analog clock on one wall read 2:20—in the afternoon, Joe assumed.

Movement in the hallway drew his attention back to the glass wall overlooking the corridor. People approached Joe's room. The door opened and in walked two men and the woman he'd seen before. The taller of the two men wore a dark gray suit and a striped tie. An FBI badge hung from a lanyard around his neck. The other man wore an FBI jacket, just like the woman's.

"Good afternoon, Mr. Pryce," said the man in the suit. His short-cropped hair showed some gray at the temples.

"My name is Senior Special Agent Deegan, and this is Special Agent Connors. You've met Field Agent Spinelli." His expressionless face and the tone of his voice suggested he meant business. "We have a couple of questions for you, so I invite you to simply relax and answer them as best you can."

"Okay," Joe responded, rather sheepishly. "But I was hoping somebody would be able to tell me where I am and how my friends are doing." Joe looked at the other agents, each of whom held blank stares. "We had also heard something about the president," he added.

"You heard something about the president?" Deegan repeated as he glanced toward the other two agents. "I'm afraid we're not at liberty to discuss any of that right now." He pulled up a chair alongside Joe's bed and pulled out a legal pad. "What I can tell you, though, is that if you can simply tell us everything about your actions during the last several hours, then I'll be more than happy to answer any questions you might have. Fair enough?"

Joe swallowed nervously. "Okay."

"Good. Now, let's begin with you giving us your full name, where you're from, and where you go to school."

"My name is George Owen Pryce, but everyone calls me Joe." He stopped and looked at each officer, finding this whole situation hard to believe. Why did this feel like an interrogation and him a suspect? Why couldn't they at least tell him how his friends were doing? And why couldn't they talk to him about the president? Even as the questions came to his mind, he could only assume they must have their reasons. He had no choice but to cooperate and answer all their questions.

"Go on."

"I live in Pennsylvania, and I go to school at Westthorpe Academy."

For the next hour, Joe answered questions about everything he had done since they first landed in California.

He shared everything he could recall, interrupted only by a nurse who checked his vital signs and brought him something to eat after realizing he hadn't had a meal in quite some time. He must have been hungrier than he realized because even though it was hospital food, he ate practically all of it.

Special Agent Deegan shifted in his chair, studying the legal pad on his lap. "I want to circle back to a couple of things." He leafed through a page or two of his notes. "You told us that after the chase down the Coast Highway, you decided it best to return to Mission San Antonio in hopes of getting help from a group of Franciscan friars you'd met there previously. Correct?"

"Yes. We couldn't get a signal on our cell phones and didn't know where else to go."

Another agent walked into the room and conferred privately with Deegan.

"Thank you," he said as the other agent turned and left the room.

Deegan gave off a rather exasperated sigh. He got up from his chair, walked to the window, and peered outside through a slit in one of the blinds. "We've done some checking at the mission," he said as he came over and stood at the foot of Joe's bed. "Turns out it's been closed for structure upgrading and restoration for the last several weeks." Deegan stopped and looked at Joe. "According to the people in charge there, no one other than a construction crew has been permitted on that property for quite some time." He paused as if waiting for Joe's reaction. "We've also made several inquiries with local, national, and even international Franciscan religious orders, none of whom knew of their members visiting Mission San Antonio anytime recently." He paused again. "You see, my friend, too many things in your story don't add up."

Joe shook his head, having no clue how to respond.

"Might I suggest you start leveling with me about where you and your friends have been these last couple of nights, what you've been doing, and who you were with?"

Joe recalled his most recent memory of the old padre talking with him as he lay on a bed in what he'd assumed was one of the rooms at the mission. But had that only been a dream or an aftereffect from the accident? He knew they had visited the mission and they had spent the last two nights there. Of that, he had no doubt.

"And that's not all," Deegan continued. "There's another matter having to do with the black bag you say your friend had with him in the back seat of the car." Deegan paused and checked his cell phone. "According to what you told us, it had been concealed in a tree next to the Whalers Cove cabin at Point Lobos."

"Yes."

"You say you were told it was payout money for the assassins."

"That's what Leo told us."

"How much money was in the bag?"

"I don't know. I never looked inside it. I think it had some kind of lock on it. It was very heavy."

"Then perhaps you can tell us the whereabouts of that bag because it was not in the car when we found you."

Joe paused. The questions came at him now like rapid fire. He wanted to be as accurate with his answers as he could, afraid if he screwed up, they would continue to hound him. The room grew noticeably warmer. The hospital gown began to stick beneath his armpits.

He tried to recall the last time he saw the bag. "I remember seeing it in the back seat the whole time. I can still picture Leo leaning on it."

"You say there was a vehicle chasing you up to the time of the accident at the mission."

"Yes." Joe stopped and thought for a moment. "Did you find out who they were? Maybe they had something to do with the missing bag."

Deegan glared at Joe. His eyes narrowed, a single eyebrow raised. A corner of his mouth tightened on one side of his face. "The only other vehicle at the scene was a US Army Military Police utility vehicle from nearby Fort Hunter Liggett. It had been tracking your car for several miles up to the time of the crash. The two MPs in the truck pulled up right after the crash and got everybody out of the car. They made no mention of seeing a black bag in their report."

"Wha—" Again, Joe hardly knew what to think or say. It had been a long and exhausting ordeal. His head ached, and a weariness slowly crept over the rest of his body.

Deegan returned to his chair. "I'm giving you a final opportunity now to tell me anything else that you may have forgotten or that you can suddenly recall about the black bag. Anything at all."

Joe tried remembering any detail he may have forgotten or had inadvertently left out, but nothing came to his mind. He looked at Special Agent Deegan. "Sir, I can honestly say I have told you everything I can remember about what happened. I know I can speak for Luke when I say neither of us had any interest in the bag and only cared about getting help, especially for Leo ... knowing how badly hurt he was." His stomach sank. How was Leo now?

Deegan gestured across the room to the other agents and pointed toward the door.

"I'll be back with more questions," he said as he turned and followed the other agents. "In the meantime, should you think of anything else you wish to tell us, Agent Spinelli will be right outside. She can get a hold of me."

Before Joe could remind Deegan of the promise he had made to answer some of his own questions, the door had already closed behind him.

Joe sighed. Things had gone from bad to worse. Not only would no one tell him anything about his friends, but now he seemed to be a suspect in an incident that may very well have brought about the demise of the president of the United States.

As his gaze shifted, he noticed a set of rosary beads on the tray near his bed. He reached with his one free hand and took hold of them—the same ones given to him by the old padre in Mission San Antonio! He immediately wanted to call out to Special Agent Deegan to show him his visit to the mission had been real. He stopped, however, when he realized that such a story would probably be difficult for someone like Deegan to believe. He hardly needed to give another reason for the FBI to raise further suspicion about him.

Though frustrated, he held the rosary beads in his hand and saw them as a sign of a renewed hope. Could there be any more important a time to pray than now? He ran his fingers over the beads and began to pray as he had never done before.

Joe opened his eyes. Turning his head, he suddenly realized the neck brace had been removed. He rubbed the upper part of his shoulders and, although a little stiff, found the soreness had gone. He looked down at his arm to see the intravenous placement no longer there.

How long had he been asleep? The clock on the wall read 8:35. Judging from the hint of light outlining the drawn blinds of the window, he guessed it must be morning. But which morning? What day? He still had no idea of the name of the hospital. And what about Luke? Why hadn't they told him anything yet? He couldn't even see the hallway on the other side of the glass wall now; someone had drawn those blinds too. At least for once, he didn't have someone watching his every move.

He pushed the sheets down and swung his legs off the bed. Planting his feet firmly on the floor, he stood up with the thought of going to the bathroom on the other side of the room. Up to that point, he had been instructed to use the various apparatuses next to his bed, not something he really liked doing.

After steadying himself, he ambled his way across the shiny linoleum to the bathroom. After finishing, he opened the door and almost jumped out of his hospital gown. A tall man wearing a dark suit and a coiled wire dangling from his ear stood staring at him from just inside the door to the room.

"Good morning. My name is Chief Security Agent Martinez of the Secret Service. We're here to inspect the room. Please remain standing where you are." He then lifted his left wrist to his mouth. "All clear."

Suddenly, the door behind him opened, and another man and a woman entered the room. The man approached Joe and asked him to spread his arms and legs apart. Joe received a thorough pat-down, similar to the one he had received at the Philadelphia Airport by the TSA before their flight to California. Though that had been just the other day, it seemed like ages ago. Joe wondered what they thought he—in nothing but a hospital gown—could possibly conceal. He struggled to keep himself decent in the thing, which seemed to be a size too small for his lanky frame.

"He's clean," the man announced to Agent Martinez.

The woman emerged from the bathroom and moved to the far side of the room. After looking around a bit more, she gave a nod to Martinez. He pivoted toward Joe. "I'm going to ask you to return to your bed if you please."

"Okay." Joe climbed back into his bed as the Secret Service agents proceeded out of the room. The door closed behind them but suddenly opened again. Joe looked up and gasped. "Couldn't be!"

CHAPTER 16

"Mr. President!" Joe's jaw dropped, his mouth gaping open, his eyes bulging out in a fixed stare.

"Hello, Joe. How are you feeling?"

The president entered the room and closed the door. No escort followed him. He wore a dark blue windbreaker jacket with the presidential seal on the right front.

Shocked, Joe hardly knew what to say. He'd been worrying about the president's health and well-being all this time—even assuming the worst. Now the president stood before him asking about *him*.

Joe scooted up in his bed. "I-I-I'm okay." He tried composing himself. "Wow!" He struggled to speak coherently. "You don't know how happy I am to see you're all right! We thought for sure you were hurt or worse."

"Well, thanks be to God, I'm still in one piece." He pulled up in the chair next to Joe's bed.

"We'd heard almost nothing ... but we kept hoping and praying."

"Well, thank you, Joe. That means a lot to me." He patted Joe's leg stretched out on the bed. "The doctor tells me you're going to be fine. You've had a slight concussion, which they've been monitoring, and a bit of whiplash. Aside from that, and a couple of bumps and bruises, he thinks you can leave the hospital soon."

"You mean I can actually get out of this place?"

"That's right—but not before I share a couple of things with you first."

"Mr. President, I can't tell you how glad I am to hear someone say that. No one's told me anything since I've been here."

"I understand—and there's been a reason for that." The president stood and walked back toward the door. "Incidentally, we've contacted your parents and have assured them that you're all right."

"Thank you." Joe thought for a moment that the president was preparing to leave. "But please don't go before telling me everything that has happened."

"Not to worry. First, I want to share something else with you." The president opened the door. Two figures stood in the doorway. Two familiar faces that Joe had longed to see more than anything else. Cheers rang out as Pete made a beeline toward Joe and hugged him.

Joe held Pete at arm's length and stared at him. "Is it really you guys?"

"You had us worried sick, dude."

"*Me?* You're the one that went running off without telling anybody."

Luke hobbled up behind Pete. He wore a sling on his left arm and a walking cast on his right foot. "Well, Pryce ... you're a sight for sore eyes."

"Hey, Luke. Man, is it great to see you're okay!" Joe got out of his bed and gently put an arm around Luke's good shoulder. "How bad is it?"

"A separated shoulder, some bruised ribs, and a sprained ankle, but other than that, I'm fine." A wry smile came to his face. "But don't think for a moment I still can't kick both your butts ... even with only one good arm."

Everybody laughed, something Joe hadn't felt much like doing of late.

Over the next several minutes, the boys laughed more and talked about everything that had happened to them.

Earlier, the president had stepped out into the hallway. Now he returned to the room. "I'm glad you all had a chance to see each other again." He strolled across the room to where the boys stood. "But now, I need a moment with Joe. Do you fellas mind waiting outside for just a couple of minutes?"

Both Luke and Pete expressed their appreciation to the president and left the room. By this time, Joe had gotten himself dressed, his clothes having been washed and returned to him. A welcome change from the less than dignified hospital gown he had been wearing. He looked at the president. "They tell me Leo isn't doing well."

The president hung his head. "Unfortunately, he's still unconscious and in critical condition. He's lost a lot of blood. The fact that he's still alive, though, says a lot about what you and Luke did for him." He glanced toward the window. "Fortunately, this hospital is only a few miles from where they found you guys." He raised his eyebrows. "And, according to what they're telling me, I may have him to thank for saving my life."

The president explained how initial reports suggested Leo risked his life to stop the assassins and how another younger man, a member of the Pebble Beach grounds crew, had warned the president just before the incident occurred. "Fortunately for me, the bullet missed its mark—but it sure did a number on my golf bag." The president offered a brief smile. "They say that had either one of them not acted, it might have been a different story."

Joe shook his head. "Not something I'd like to think about." Joe had spent enough time worrying about the president and didn't want to have to think about that possibility again.

"We have much to be thankful for, my friend. You and I both share a common faith that believes Divine Providence plays a part in all things." The president lowered his eyes and shook his head. "You can imagine my shock and surprise when I heard your name mentioned and the extent to which you and your friends got caught up in this thing." He looked at Joe. "And when I think about the risks both you and Luke took to help someone the way you did ... it was nothing short of an extraordinary act of courage and selflessness—something, let us hope and pray, Leo can ultimately thank you personally for."

"I hope so, too." Joe wished there had been something more he and Luke could have done for Leo. He seemed like a decent enough guy. How he had gotten involved in all this, he couldn't imagine. All he could do now was continue praying for him and hoping for the best.

The president looked at his phone and began tapping something on it.

Joe thought back to the weekend spent last year with Pete and their families at Camp David at the invitation of the president. It was a more carefree time compared to what they were going through now.

"Aside from my obvious concern for you and your friends, Joe, let me also share something else with you." He paused, sliding his phone back into his pocket. "Based on what you and Luke have said in your statements, there's a strong possibility the two bodies found at the bottom of the ravine beneath Bixby Canyon Bridge were the same men who chased you and may also have been the ones involved in the assassination attempt—but we don't know that for sure."

Joe recalled the terrifying scene in his mind of the pickup truck falling beneath the bridge. Regardless of who those men might have been, nobody deserved to meet their end that way.

"Unfortunately, the bodies were burned beyond recognition, and it may take quite a while before a positive identification can be made on either one, if at all." The president paused. "Strangely, the young man I mentioned earlier from the grounds crew at Pebble Beach has been identified as having possible Russian connections. His older brother works for a company with holdings in Russia and had helped him get the job at the golf course. Some think that information about my visit there might have been relayed from someone on the course to the people responsible for the shooting."

The president pulled up one end of a sleeve of his jacket and checked his watch. "The problem right now, Joe, is if Leo's condition doesn't improve, he may not be able to tell us anything beyond what he has told you and Luke." He took out his phone again and scrolled through it. "We do know his full name is Leonid Verenich. He came here from Russia some years ago and has since gained legal permanent residence status here in the US."

Joe could see the strain beginning to wear on the president. He looked like he hadn't slept much recently, noticeable circles had formed beneath his eyes. His hair had turned grayer since the last time Joe had seen him in person at Camp David just about a year ago.

"As of now, none of this has been shared with the public—not an easy thing to do, considering how the media is abuzz with all sorts of wild speculation and conjecture." He rubbed his furrowed brow. "But we need to start getting answers and getting them quickly before there's talk of how this could be the start of World War III. That explains why the FBI had to be particularly tough with their questions with both you and Luke."

"I completely understand, Mr. President." As uncomfortable as the interview had gone with the FBI, Joe now realized how their methods may have been necessary.

"Before we can start pointing fingers at anyone, though, we need more facts at our disposal. Otherwise, the minute word of Russian involvement gets out, be it their government or some rogue operation within their country, it will only result in denials and obfuscations from their end." An increased pitch in the president's voice gave an indication of growing frustration.

"The truth is until Leo Verenich can tell us something, and there's a distinct possibility he may not ever be able to do that, the whereabouts of the black bag becomes even more critical." The president gazed directly at Joe. "If it is the payout money, as both you and Luke say Leo described it, it could give us what we need to track the money to its source."

The president sighed. "And that's the primary reason I'm here." He stopped and checked his phone again. "To tell you the truth, the FBI is breathing down my neck about this." He raised a hand and pointed toward the door of the room. "They do their job well, but they tell me they're having a difficult time believing what you and Luke are telling them."

A tension had suddenly entered the room. Joe had always trusted and admired the president as a man of great faith, something Joe witnessed personally from the moment he first met him. But he also realized the enormous pressures he fell under. The president had to face the realities of an often hostile and cynical world. Given the current situation, he needed immediate answers to questions being pressed upon him by the media. No doubt, he also needed to assure the people of the United States and the people and governments of nations throughout the world that the situation was under control and that there was no reason to panic.

"To be honest, Joe, when the FBI briefed me on the situation here, it was obvious to me that they felt somebody wasn't being forthright enough."

The president stopped. He gazed across the room, his eyes fixed on something near Joe's bed. Joe watched curiously as the president strode toward the overbed table. "What an extraordinary set of rosary beads," he said, his voice suddenly calm and relaxed.

Joe had almost forgotten about the rosary beads. He grabbed them from the table and handed them to the president.

"These are quite beautiful." The president ran them through his fingers. "I don't know that I've ever seen anything like them." He studied the beads more closely. "You know, I take great pride in having received rosary beads as a gift from the pope during my trip to Rome earlier this year. But ... I must admit ... as much as I cherish those, there is something unique about these. They seem to have a fascinating history to them." He handed them back to Joe. "May I ask where you got them?"

Joe hesitated. If he answered honestly, he'd be disclosing something to the president that he hadn't shared in his previous statements to the FBI. But he also knew he and the president could speak honestly with one another about their shared faith, going back to the extraordinary events from last year involving Joe's school and their visit to Camp David.

Joe proceeded to tell the president everything about the old padre, beginning with that first night at the Mission San Antonio chapel. He explained how he saw him again after the accident in what seemed more like a dream. "I guess that's why I never mentioned it before."

The president remained silent for a moment. "I can hardly fault you for that. I probably would have done the same thing."

Joe shared how he received the rosary beads from the padre, who told him they had been given to him by an Indian family from the Mission at San Carlos Borromeo in Carmel. In both instances, Joe recounted how the padre emphasized the need to pray and trust in God if we truly desire to have peace in the world.

Joe opened his hand and gazed once more at the beads resting in his palm. "Only when I saw them again did I know for certain the experience had been real."

The president nodded his head. His eyes narrowed as if he were deep in thought. Joe knew that the supernatural nature of what he revealed to the president had not been anything unfamiliar to either of them. But whether from past events or now, Joe had come to see them as occasions of extraordinary grace. Perhaps on this occasion, though, the stakes were much higher.

"Thank you, Joe, for sharing this with me." The president stepped toward the window. "These last couple of days have proven once again how fragile and perilous life can sometimes be." He peered through the blinds to the world outside. "History is a great teacher filled with stories of human greatness and achievement, as well as tragedy and despair." He paused. "And when misfortune strikes, it is easy to become despondent and lose heart in the face of adversity." He turned and pointed to the rosary beads, which Joe had returned to the table. "But we can also rise to meet those challenges and, with God's help, find a way to overcome them."

The president turned, crossed the room again, and picked up the rosary beads. "No doubt you've become pretty familiar with St. Junipero Serra, Joe. He's a saint for our times, for sure. His legacy ... it's quite extraordinary, enshrined forever in the missions he founded." The president dropped his gaze and shook his head. "Sadly, he's been quite a bit misunderstood of late, but his legacy is a part of our own heritage." The president opened Joe's hand and placed the rosary beads in the center of his palm. "I like to think St. Junipero Serra is reminding us of our responsibility to be a voice of peace in the world. He certainly knew something himself about bringing people of different cultures, races, and languages together as children of the same God."

The president leaned against the footboard of Joe's bed. "It's not hard to see, Joe, the similar challenges we face today. Yes, there is plenty of hostility and discord in the world, but I'm convinced Father Serra is encouraging us to be strong and to trust in God through prayer and self-sacrifice."

Joe gripped the beads in his hand, greatly encouraged by the president's words.

A subtle grin creased the president's lips. "This has certainly given me something to think about." He paused. "In fact, it has inspired me enough to say that, against what is probably the better advice of my senior staff, I have every intention of attending Wednesday's event at the Carmel Mission for the dedication of the bell and to honor St. Junipero Serra, regardless of what news may come from yesterday's incident."

A knock at the door brought a member of the president's staff into the room. "Sir, we've just received news on the condition of the patient, Leonid Verenich."

"How is he?" the president asked.

"The doctor wants you to come right away. He wouldn't say anything more."

The president jumped up. "This doesn't sound good." He followed his aide from the room as the door closed behind him.

CHAPTER 17

The sun shone brightly, and a gentle breeze cooled the warm air on this beautiful California afternoon. Joe shielded his eyes as the sunlight illumined the sandstone walls of the Carmel Mission Basilica and reflected off the glass of a spectacular star-shaped window just above the entrance.

"You know this church is one of the most authentically restored of all the missions." Father Nowakowski walked just ahead of Joe, Father Al, Luke, and Pete as they approached the front of the chapel. "And this is the only one of the California missions to still have its original bell tower dome." Joe listened with a curious fascination, enjoying another history lesson from Father Nowa.

Father Nowa stopped and looked up. "Both the window and the oval-shaped dome reflect a unique style of architecture the Spanish brought with them to the Americas—a style greatly influenced by the Moors who dominated most of Spain for many centuries." Father paused and took a swig from his water bottle. "The Moors brought their Muslim religion with them, which became interwoven with the culture of Catholic Spain, creating a unique blend that shaped many aspects of life including the architecture that you see on display here."

Father Nowa pointed high above them. "Unfortunately, though, you'll notice the lack of bells in the bell towers."

Joe gazed up, noticing two different towers on each side of a round-arched elevation directly above the front doorway. The dome had a cross on top and rested above the larger bell tower to the left. He peered through the openings in both belfries only to confirm what Father Nowa had described—no bells hung in either of the bell towers.

"What's a Spanish mission without its bells?" Pete squinted as he arched his neck skyward to get a better view. "I know we're here to rededicate one that had been lost, but did the same happen to all of them?"

"Great questions, Pete." Father Nowa nodded. "Unfortunately, this mission also suffered damage from vandals some weeks ago, including the bells that had been in the towers. They've since been removed for repairs. The original plan had been to ring them as part of today's ceremony."

Heightened security could be seen everywhere around the Carmel Mission. As he had promised, the president insisted that the Mass and ceremony take place as scheduled and that he would attend.

The group made their way through the gauntlet of metal detectors, pat-downs, and other security measures. Once within the mission walls, they walked through the mission's beautiful courtyard and gardens before stopping in the cemetery. Joe noticed the gravesites of Indians buried alongside those of Franciscan friars and others who had lived and worked at the mission—some as old as the mission itself.

The doors of the church opened, and people began to proceed inside. Father Nowa led Father Al and the boys through the entrance. "This is actually considered a *basilica,* which is the highest honorary title given to certain churches."

Joe marveled at the interior of the basilica. It featured high-reaching arches that formed an inverted U-shaped vaulted ceiling—a style Father Nowa had described as *catenary*. Beautiful works of religious art and statuary adorned the walls on each side of the single-center aisle. Behind the main altar stood an elaborately designed and colorfully decorated back wall with a large crucifix and several statues of saints positioned symmetrically between columns and alcoves. The lower center of the wall held the tabernacle, gold-plated and partially obscured by a thin, gold-colored veil.

A Secret Service agent signaled for their group to move toward the front of the church. They had all been given lanyards that indicated where they would be sitting. As they approached, Joe could see a portrait of Junipero Serra facing toward the congregation, positioned on a stand along the floor near the steps leading up to the sanctuary—the same image Joe had seen at the conference the other day.

The saint's burial place lay beneath the floor just before the portrait, marked by a simple flat stone with the inscription: *Fr. Junipero Serra, Apostol de California, 1713—1784*.

After genuflecting, they settled into their pew and knelt in prayer, preparing for the celebration of Holy Mass. Organ music played softly behind them from the choir loft above the front entrance. The soothing music helped put Joe into a reflective repose.

What a last couple of days it had been. He prayed in thanksgiving for the protection he and his friends had received throughout the harrowing ordeal. He gave thanks for the safety and well-being of the president. The more discoveries made about the incident, the more people became convinced that divine intervention had played a direct hand in preventing what could have been an unspeakable tragedy.

He gave thanks for the continued improvement of Leo Verenich, who, although he had not been doing well at first, had since made a rather miraculous recovery. As much as his condition remained serious, he had been able to answer questions and provide valuable information. Strangely though, the whereabouts of the black bag still remained a mystery.

Evidence strongly pointed to Usenko Enterprises as having conspired with some Russian oligarchs, businessmen, and elements within *Bratva*—the Russian mafia. A California-based crime syndicate named *AP-13*, tied to Russian organized crime, appeared to have been directly involved. Together, they had set out to bring down an American president who they felt jeopardized their financial interests through the imposition of economic sanctions upon their country.

Having earlier contacted the president to inquire as to his well-being, President Tarasovich of Russia assured him that the Russian government had nothing to do with what had happened and promised his full cooperation in helping find those responsible and bringing them to justice.

To the surprise and consternation of many of his advisers, the president welcomed Russia's offer of assistance and extended to them his sincere gratitude. He went even further by inviting the Russian president to come immediately to California so, together, they could sit down and discuss solutions to their differences for the good of their two countries and the sake of world peace. He also reminded him that the original plan had been for both presidents of their countries to meet that week in Carmel for the dedication of the recovered bell that had been a gift from Russia to the mission so many years ago.

Sudden applause from the rear of the church yanked Joe from his quiet introspection. He turned to look behind him. The crowd watched as the presidents of both the United States and Russia, together with their first ladies, walked down the center aisle. They proceeded to the opposite side of the aisle and took their places in the front pew.

The music of an inspiring hymn signaled the start of Mass. The procession, led by altar servers carrying a golden crucifix and two large candles, made its way up the center aisle and toward the sanctuary. Several priests, some wearing the habits of their Franciscan order, followed closely behind, the last being the Bishop of the Diocese of Monterey wearing a mitered hat and carrying his shepherd's staff.

Joe found himself transfixed by the reverence and devotion of the Mass celebration. He sensed that due to much of what had happened the last couple of days, the people of the congregation also experienced a deeper awareness and appreciation of the need for prayer and reflection in their lives. Not only that, but each person there also witnessed a profound hope for the world as they watched both presidents sitting side by side in a shared fellowship and worship of God.

After Mass, everyone moved into the large courtyard for the blessing and dedication of the Russian bell. It hung from a simple stand near a large wooden cross that marked the very spot where Father Serra had first established the mission some two hundred and fifty years ago.

Joe listened as the bishop spoke of the wonderful occasion that had brought them all together that day. It was an opportunity, he explained, not only to celebrate the life and work of Junipero Serra but to remind the world of the need for all people to come together in a shared desire for peace and goodwill among all nations.

After sprinkling the bell with holy water and offering a prayer of blessing, the bishop invited both presidents to approach the bell. They each took hold of the rope cord connected to the striker and, with one pull, rang the bell.

As the people applauded, a loud and sudden burst of sound fell upon them in the courtyard, like a clap of thunder from the sky. Startled at first, Joe turned his head up in the direction of the bell towers. Earlier, he had seen for himself how the towers held no bells in them. But what he now saw astounded him. He lowered his head momentarily and rubbed his eyes, trying to make certain they didn't deceive him. Peering up again, he could clearly see bells ringing in the belfries, each with a striker pulled by a rope—their sound reverberating throughout the mission grounds and beyond.

Joe turned and found Father Nowa, his eyes widened in a blank stare. Joe could barely hear him as he tried to speak. "How can this be?" His voice trembled. "How could the bells have been reinstalled so quickly? It's impossible!"

Joe glanced from left to right among the crowd in the courtyard. Most of the people stared upward, their mouths gaping open in stunned amazement. He soon noticed something else beginning to happen. As he listened to the bells, Joe became enraptured by their beautiful and sublime resonance—unlike anything he had ever heard before. They rang with a magnificent union of harmonized notes, tones, and pitches so perfectly in tune as to be something from beyond this world. Many in the crowd who had recovered from the initial shock raised their arms in joyful praise, their heads tilted toward the heavens, some with tears in their eyes. Joe looked at Father Nowa, Father Al, Luke, and Pete, each reaching out to one another in a shared exuberance and euphoria.

Joe raised his head again toward the bells. Bright sunlight broke through the clouds, temporarily blinding him. He shielded his eyes as he peered into the bell tower. Through the glare, he could just make out several figures, some pulling on the ropes of the bells, others descending the outside steps to the left of the tower leading to the belfry.

As Joe's eyes gradually adjusted to the light, the figures became more distinct. He could now see Indian men, women, and children, all dressed in traditional clothing, descending from the outside of the tower, together with several Franciscan friars.

Pete pointed toward the belltower. "Those are the friars we saw at Mission San Antonio. And that's the Indian boy I saw on the beach near the rocks at China Grove, along with the other men in the cave I told you about!" He glanced at Joe, a widening grin on his face. "Now, do you believe me?"

But Joe didn't reply as he strained to see if he could find the old padre. Suddenly a figure appeared, standing at the top of the steps. The old padre gazed out beyond the crowd as if looking into the surrounding woods and hills, or perhaps the entire world, beckoning all to come to the mission. "Come, oh come, my children, to this holy place!" he cried out, his arms raised. "Come and share in the peace and love of God! All are welcome!"

Joe continued to shield his eyes as the sunlight remained intensely bright. He watched as the other friars gathered with the Indians in the courtyard at the foot of the steps. The old padre raised his right hand toward the people and offered his priestly blessing with the Sign of the Cross. He then descended the steps and joined the Indians and his brother friars. A host of radiant winged figures surrounded them as they turned and walked together in the direction of the sun, gradually disappearing into the light.

"Thank you, Father Serra," Joe whispered. "And please pray for us."

Suddenly, a cloud moved across the sun, and a peaceful calm settled upon the gathering in the courtyard. The celestial sound of the bells could no longer be heard. Joe peered up into the tower's belfry only to find it as it was before—without its bells.

CHAPTER 18

Joe lay in bed, a couple of pillows stacked behind his head and J.R.R. Tolkien's *Lord of the Rings: The Fellowship of the Ring* propped open and resting on top of his chest. His mother told him he had put off his English Lit summer reading assignment for far too long. In fact, she insisted he have the first section of the review questions completed by the end of the day. School would be starting in a couple of weeks, and he still had plenty of work to do.

His phone buzzed on the nightstand.

PETE: HEY, I'LL DRIVE US TO THE GAME. GOT TO TELL YOU SOMETHING. BE OVER LATER.

Joe had gotten so involved in his assignment he'd almost forgotten about tonight's ballgame—their last baseball game of the summer. Coach told him he would probably be pitching, so he needed to be ready. But if he didn't get these questions done, his mother wouldn't let him play.

Pete told him he had something to tell him. He wondered what it could be. He took his laptop out and started looking at the review questions, but his mind wandered. It had only been a few short weeks since they returned home from California. Joe could hardly have imagined the trip turning out the way it did. In the days and weeks following the extraordinary event at the Carmel Mission, none of the people who witnessed it could say they didn't take something from the experience that changed their lives forever.

Many already called it a miracle. Some chose to speak openly about what they had seen and heard, while others preferred to keep it more private. Several members of the secular media who attended the event had a difficult time trying to explain something they did not understand or, for that matter, believe. But they could hardly ignore what they experienced with their own eyes and ears or the accounts of the dozens of people who had visited the mission that day. Regardless, it certainly seemed to have a profound effect on the presidents from both the United States and Russia—in the days that followed, they wasted little time in sitting down and discussing ways of settling disputes between their two countries. Together they reached an agreement on an accord that would work toward resolving those differences and putting the world on a more secure footing toward global peace.

Meanwhile, a full-fledged investigation to find those responsible for the attempt on the president's life had already begun in earnest. The inquiry would ultimately involve the International Court of Justice of the United Nations, as well as the mutual cooperation of the governments of the United States and Russia.

Although several months would be required to bring to justice all those involved in the conspiracy, it became clear early on how mitigating circumstances would play a large part in reducing and even removing the responsibility of some of those connected to the incident. The president went out of his way to thank Nick Antonovich for his heroic actions in warning him at the golf course. Nick pleaded the case for his brother Yuri, who swore he knew nothing of the plot to bring harm to the president. However, due to some of his shady business dealings, it took some considerable doing before Yuri was exonerated, resulting in a joyful reunion not only with Nick but with their father.

"Joe, dear, I'm running out to the store," his mom called from downstairs. "I want to see some of your work when I get back."

"Ugh," Joe said to himself.

"Did you hear me, sweety?"

"Yes, Mom."

"Oh, and there's a letter here for you in the mail I meant to tell you about. I'll leave it on the table in the foyer."

A letter? Strange. Who could be writing him a letter?

"Okay, thanks."

Who wrote letters these days? Who could it be from? Joe kept working for a few minutes but finally decided he needed to find out. Frodo Baggins and the Ringwraiths would have to wait.

He scampered down the stairs and found the letter, his name and address neatly handwritten on the envelope. The return address gave no name but had a Salinas, California, street address. As far as he knew, he didn't know anyone from there. He had met a lot of people on the trip but couldn't think of anybody who might be writing him.

Joe ventured into the kitchen and grabbed a bottled water from the refrigerator. He settled into a chair in the breakfast nook, anxious to open the letter. Suddenly, the doorbell rang. Who could that be? Must be one of Mom's deliveries from Amazon. Joe got up and moved toward the front door. Halfway across the atrium, the door swung open, and in sauntered Pete, partially dressed in his baseball uniform.

"Hey, buddy. What's up?" He shut the door behind him.

"Nice of you to make yourself at home, Figueroa."

"Thought I'd come by a little early and check out some pregame snacks you might have."

The two made their way into the kitchen. Pete opened the refrigerator and peered inside. Joe sat back down and began tearing into the envelope.

"Hey, this looks good." Pete lifted a container of leftover chicken nuggets from the top shelf and threw it into the microwave. "Have I got some news for you." After a few seconds, he opened the microwave and carried the chicken nuggets over to the table. "Got any sauce?"

Joe pointed toward the refrigerator. "Inside the door, second shelf." He hesitated with the letter for a moment. "Yeah, I figured you'd get around to telling me at some point."

Pete sat down in the chair next to Joe and dipped a nugget in some honey mustard. "I didn't want to interrupt your letter opening over here."

"Not a problem." He put the letter down. "It can wait. Besides, I want to hear the news."

"No. I insist. Who's the letter from? A secret admirer? Anybody I know?" He grabbed another chicken nugget and popped it in his mouth.

"It's from California."

"Oh." Pete's eyes widened. "Then you have to read it now." He got up, opened the refrigerator, and grabbed a cherry cola from the bottom shelf. "Maybe it's from one of the girls we met at the beach."

"Yeah, right." Joe rolled his eyes. "You mean the ones you tried to impress with stories about finding gold? I don't think so." He picked up the letter again, happy to finally be able to discover its contents. He removed a typed letter from the envelope, along with a copy of a newspaper article. He opened the letter and glanced down at the handwritten signature at the bottom. A smile came to his face. "It's from Leo Verenich."

"No kidding." Pete popped open the soda can. "Read it out loud for us."

Joe paused. They had received almost no news about Leo since leaving California. After taking a serious turn for the worse, not long after being brought to the same hospital where Joe and Luke had been treated, he made what his doctor called a *miraculous* recovery. The president also spoke highly of Leo, who risked his life to save him. But because of his previous connections with those directly involved in the conspiracy, it would take longer to determine his ultimate fate.

Both Joe and Luke made determined efforts to help Leo in their statements. Joe had come to admire Leo for not only risking his own life to protect the president but for what he had done to keep Adrik Chernov from getting away. Joe prayed for Leo's recovery and had worried when there had been little news about him. But now, he had a letter from him.

Dear Joe,

Hoping you, Luke, and Pete are all doing well after getting home to Pennsylvania. Seeing as I'm not much at sending texts or using other social media, I thought I'd write you this letter. I'm doing much better. They tell me I should be able to have full use of my arm and shoulder with some physical therapy.

I can't thank you and Luke enough for what you both did in helping save my life and for your kind words in supporting me. Thank you also for your prayers. I really felt them when things weren't going so well. This whole thing has given me a lot to think about with my own life and my relationship with the Almighty. I heard about what happened at the Carmel Mission. One day, I would very much like to sit down and have you tell me all about it.

I'm under a sort of house arrest with a no-fly restriction. For how long, I'm not sure. The good news is I've been given enough assurances that I don't think they'll be bringing any charges against me. I have you, Luke, and the president to thank for that.

I've included a copy of an article from one of our local newspapers for you to look at.

Joe unfolded the other page.

"What's that?" Pete asked.

"He included a copy of a newspaper article." The heading over a rather short article announced, *Missions Given Largest-Ever Donation*. Joe scanned the story. "It talks about how the California Missions Foundation received a mysterious gift of six million dollars from an anonymous donor." Joe read further down. "The money was given to help fund projects to protect and preserve the future of the missions. It's the largest donation they've ever received."

"That's great," Pete said. "I remember hearing on the trip how a lot of the missions were in serious need of expensive repairs."

All good news, Joe thought, but he figured there had to be another reason why Leo would tell him all this. He put the article aside and looked at the letter again.

> As you know, the money from the black bag has never been found. I'm also told the two bodies under Bixby Bridge were burned beyond recognition and may never be identified. Some are saying both Chernov and Sergei Pacenko are still alive and somehow made off with the money.
>
> I've had trouble sleeping at night, knowing they could still be out there. But ever since hearing of the mission donation, I am convinced it's the same money that was in the black bag! Think about it. The money was donated from an anonymous source. Six million dollars is exactly the kind of payout Adrik Chernov would have demanded for a high-priced target. Not to mention the timing of it all. It's enough to convince me.
>
> If anything, it at least gives me a good feeling to know the lost money has somehow been put to good use after all. It also helps in assuring me both Chernov and Pacenko have met their

Maker. God works in strange ways, Joe, and I like to think this is another one of those times. Please keep praying for me that all of this will be over soon. Give my best to Luke and Pete. I am forever grateful for what all of you have done for me.

I hope our paths will cross again someday soon. Until then, may God bless you always.

Your friend,
Leo Verenich

"Wow!" Pete sat back in his chair. "Do you think he's right about the money? Do you think it's possible?"

"Hey, we've both seen stranger things." Joe reached over and grabbed a nugget for himself. "The donor went out of their way to remain anonymous, which means we may never know for sure."

Pete got up again and helped himself to a bottled water from the bottom of the refrigerator. "I might bring this for the game if that's all right."

"Sure. Is there anything else I can get for you?" Joe looked at Pete, his eyebrows raised, hardly believing his friend's run of the house. "Don't they feed you over at your place?"

Pete took the cap off the bottle. "I'm good for now—thanks." He sat back down. "You know, this is actually the perfect segue to the news I had."

"Glad to hear. It's about time we got to it." Joe sat up, eager to listen.

"Well, I've also been thinking about ways of helping the missions." He took a swig from his drink and wiped his mouth with the back of his hand. "I've been making plans for our next trip to California."

"You don't say?" Joe took another nugget, noticing how few remained after watching Pete eat most of them.

"There's plenty of gold in that cave I visited to help provide for the missions." Pete reached for the last nugget and dipped it in the sauce. "And maybe just a little to take home for ourselves."

"Just a little, huh?"

"Don't forget, I had some of that gold in my own hands." He opened his arms and extended them out. "I only wish I had held onto it."

Joe shook his head. "Yeah, and don't forget how you fell on the rocks and could have been seriously hurt. Not to mention we couldn't find you."

"Come on, I was fine." Pete pulled out his phone. "How does next Christmas break sound?" He scrolled down on the screen. "I've been in touch with Luke, and we've been looking at some flights. I can let him know we're coming."

"This was the big news you came over to tell me?" Joe got up and placed an empty glass in the sink. "You know, Pete, I think I might like staying home for a while longer before our next adventure, wherever that might be." He returned to his chair and raised his arms behind him, resting his head on the palms of his hands. "Besides, plenty of other places are out there to explore that we haven't been to yet." He smiled. "Maybe something a little closer to home might be nice."

He touched the Saint George medal around his neck and then felt for the rosary beads in his pants pocket—the ones given to him by the old padre. He turned and gazed out the kitchen window, comforted by the thought that no matter the time or the place, he could always count on friends in high places, looking out for them wherever they went.

Saint Junipero Serra, pray for us!

ABOUT THE AUTHOR

Joseph Lewis lives in Exton, Pennsylvania, with his wife Marian. They are blessed with six grown children and two granddaughters.

Aside from his writing, Joe teaches history at Regina Luminis Academy in Berwyn, Pennsylvania. He is a graduate of Villanova University, holds a masters in theology from the Graduate School of Theology at Christendom College, and has done doctoral work in theology at Catholic University.

His first book, *The Ghosts of Westthorpe Academy*, was published in 2018.

www.ingramcontent.com/pod-product-compliance
Lightning Source LLC
Chambersburg PA
CBHW070839030726
47504CB00005B/1159
9781649495679